I0676254

Also By Adam Cesare

Tribesmen

Video Night

The Summer Job

The First One You Expect

Exponential

Mercy House

Zero Lives Remaining

Collections

Bone Meal Broth

Collaborations

All-Night Terror (w/ Matt Serafini)

Jackpot (w/ Shane McKenzie, David Bernstein, Kristopher Rufty)

Bottom Feeders (w/ Cameron Pierce)

Crawling Darkness (w/ Cameron Pierce)

Copyright © Adam Cesare, 2016

Cover by George Cotronis

Copyediting by J. David Osborne

Interior Layout by Scott Cole

Black T-Shirt Books Logo by Chris Enterline

All rights reserved

This book is a work of fiction. Names, characters, places, and incidents are either products of the author's imagination or are used fictitiously. Any resemblance to actual events, locales, or persons, living or dead, is entirely coincidental. No part of this publication may be reproduced or transmitted in any form or by any means, electronic or mechanical, without written permission from the author.

For more information about the author and to get
a FREE ebook of short stories for signing up for his mailing list,
visit www.adamcesare.com

THE CON SEASON

by Adam Cesare

"It's good to see you again, my homicidal friends."

-William Castle

On The Road

Keith Lumbra squinted against the strobe of the cop light and rolled to a stop.

Unlike half the stop signs and red lights over the weekend, this time he remembered he was hauling a trailer. He slowed to a stop, administering a slight pressure to the brake to ensure that all his shit didn't go flying.

Keith hadn't been speeding and he wasn't drunk—merely maintaining a light post-con buzz—so he figured it was his out-of-state plates getting him into trouble.

That there was no reason didn't stop his asshole from irising into nonexistence.

Keith hated cops. Always had and always would. He had no good philosophical reason to dislike them. He wasn't a minority, and didn't hold any strong political beliefs outside of his Lloyd Kaufman-inspired pseudo-anarchist leanings.

He may have had no good ideological reason to dislike cops, but he did have one pretty good anecdotal one:

Ten years ago, early in his career, Keith had to cross the US-Canadian border to get to his first convention in Toronto. Back in those days, MOD, Manufacture on Demand, hadn't been a thing. Which meant that it had been an expensive undertaking to order two hundred copies of his first film on DVD. It was so expensive that he'd opted to use a hair dryer to do the shrink wrapping himself, rather than pay the extra fee.

At the customs inspection booth, when asked if he had anything to declare, he didn't say "no" like every American except him *apparently* knew to do. Instead he told the customs official, somewhat haughtily, that: yes, in his trunk he was hauling two hundred copies of his first feature film.

Apparently, the Canadian government isn't as liberal as they want people to think. Either that or the officers couldn't grasp the layers of psychosexual satire at work in the title and back cover description for a movie called *Teenage Cumsluts in Tortureland*.

Long story short: Keith Lumbra wasn't able to sell any DVDs in Toronto. It was cool, though. He may have taken the hit at the convention (where he was still able to sign and distribute postcards), but the coverage of the customs seizure itself had gotten him great press. His best coverage to date, actually, with what seemed like half of the horror community drawing comparisons between the Canadian confiscation of his movie and Ruggero Deodato's famed court appearance to prove that he hadn't actually killed his actors while filming *Cannibal Holocaust*.

Silver lining aside, at the time not being able to sell his movie had been a nightmare.

But that was then and this was now. He wouldn't blow it with these cops. These American cops.

Using the door's power controls to angle his side mirror as far away from the car as he could, Keith strained to see the cop car from behind his U-Haul trailer.

No matter how he craned his neck, he couldn't make out much in the quickening darkness.

It didn't seem late enough to be dark, but Keith reminded himself that he was out in the country. Without the benefit of a strip mall on both sides of the road, there was no light pollution to extend the day. Out here in the boonies, the transition from dusk to night happened quickly.

There was the crunch of boot heels against gravel and Keith still couldn't see anything, just the blink of the single blue strobe.

The knock came on the passenger's side window, not the driver's side.

The clatter of the metal flashlight against glass was not inherently terrifying, but it was loud and unexpected.

It was a well-executed jump-scare that—if it were in a movie— Keith Lumbra would have admired. The noise put the terror into Keith by taking advantage of both surprise and misdirection.

"Roll your window down, sir." Keith could make out the cop's voice, the words slightly muffled by the glass.

He did as he was told.

"License and papers, please," the cop asked, the light of the flashlight still blinding Keith.

Fucker must love this, Keith thought, his mood stabilizing. He shielded his eyes against the flashlight so he could fish out and then flip open his wallet.

After a weekend of crawling the convention floor and marinating in the hotel bar of the Indianapolis East Courtyard Marriott, Keith almost handed the cop his business card by virtue of muscle memory. *The name's Keith Lumbra, I make fucked-up splatter flicks.* He was glad he didn't regurgitate his rehearsed sales pitch.

The cop barely glanced at the license before saying: "You're a long way from New Jersey, Mr. Goldman. Mind if we ask why?"

Hearing his legal name, not Keith Lumbra but Keith Goldman, always threw Keith off. But it sometimes served as a reminder that he had been doing the right thing when he adopted a pseudonym. The cop's anti-Semitic emphasis on the 'O' in Goldman wasn't in his imagination.

Wait, what 'we'? Keith thought, decoding what the cop had said. Mind if *we* ask... There was more than one cop out there?

Keith turned to look in the driver's mirror again and found it blocked by the second cop's crotch. He'd been flanked without ever hearing the second cop approach. The second man was leaning so close to the car that Keith couldn't see anything above his elbows. Ninja cop was so tall and so close that he had no face.

There was a painful bubble of indigestion kicking around in Keith's gut that hadn't been there before, less a Flaming Hot Cheeto fart than it was an anxiety pang aided and abetted by Flaming Hot Cheetos.

Keith spoke as he leaned over in his seat, reaching for the glove compartment to fish out his registration. Or his "papers" like the cop had called them, fascist allusion be damned.

"Uh, I was attending a trade show. A convention. Over the weekend in Indy," Keith said. He tried to keep his diction formal and his actual business in Indianapolis oblique. His intestines torsed a second time. Something shifted as he stretched his arm to hand the cop at the window his pink slip.

There was a long pause as the man crinkled the papers, presumably reading.

While waiting, Keith looked straight forward. He could feel the cool air from the open window begin to dry the sweat gathering in his eyebrows. In his peripheral vision, Keith noticed something odd. The cop to his left wasn't wearing uniform pants, but instead what looked from this angle like black denim jeans.

Keith had owned a pair of black jeans in high school, but even then he'd been a special case. Who wore black denim these days? And how were these cops allowed to do so on duty?

This thought was interrupted by the cop with the flashlight. "Wait, you don't mean you were at that *horror* convention they've got up there, do you?" the cop asked. There was a smile in the man's voice.

Instantly, Keith felt better.

No non-fan pronounced the word 'horror' like this guy just did. Normals, people not into the genre, always over-annunciated the word to make sure it didn't sound like they were saying "whore." Either that or they dodged the quandary entirely by referring to horror flicks as "scary movies." The same phrase a child would use.

"Yup," Keith said, and then he pushed in all his chips: "I'm a filmmaker, actually. I was there repping my production company."

"Get out of town! My partner was just there, too, weren't you Benny?" the cop said, still not taking the flashlight from where it rested against the window. At least now Keith's eyes had begun to adjust.

Instead of speaking, Benny just gave an "Mmm-hhhmmm" that Keith wouldn't have been able to hear if the cop in the black jeans had not been standing two inches from the car.

"Is that what you've got back in the hitch?" Window Cop asked.

"Yes sir, just some props and displays, a few banners." Keith said, overjoyed that the words "do you know how fast you were going?" or "step out of the car, please" hadn't yet been spoken, and didn't seem like they would be. These cops seemed nice, downright chummy.

"You don't say?" The cop paused. Now *he* sounded like the nervous one. "Well. Mr. Goldman, I hate to be bothering you like this, but Benny got to go to the convention and I didn't. Would you mind showing me what you've got back there? Just a quick peek."

Uh oh.

Now Keith was searching for excuses as a nightmare scenario similar to his Canadian adventure began to play itself out in his imagination.

The cop had an accent, it was that weird bump up against Southern and Midwestern that you found as you traveled with any depth into the eastern half of the country. In movies, at least, that accent almost always accompanied a religious bend, sometimes a fundamentalist furor. Keith thought of that and then considered what he had in the U-Haul. He wasn't toting around rubber Frankenstein masks and those plastic garbage bag ghosts that you hang on your trees during October. No. He was a *modern* horror director, someone who made transgressive films.

There was some real sickness back in the trailer: A girl's severed head with her nipples stapled over her eyes. A torso that had a series of holes bored into it, the uses for the holes not a mystery if you thought about their circumference for too long. Not to mention a box full of erotic comics that he'd traded a few of his own DVDs for in the vendor's room. The comics weren't anything that he had creative involvement with, but still: they were pretty extreme.

The silent cop, Benny, had attended the convention and was probably cool with anything, but how much of a horror fan was his partner? Could he roll hard into the gore shit?

"I guess I can show you, but I do have to warn you officer that it's not for the faint of heart. Some of it's pretty gross."

"Oh never mind that," the cop waved the flashlight. "I can handle it. Seen all those *Saw* movies. And it won't take us but a minute and then we'll have you on your way."

Nothing the man had just said put Keith at ease. Those were mainstream movies.

Keith said okay and then shut off his engine, realizing he needed the key ring to open the hitch. There was that crack of gravel again, in stereo, as both cops walked back to the trailer.

Without the dashboard lights there was just the single blue police light spinning. It struck Keith as odd that the cops didn't have their own headlights on. And even odder that they didn't have a red light to accompany the blue one.

He double-checked that the car was in park, not wanting to become a YouTube sensation if he left it in neutral and the cops had a dashboard cam. He then hefted himself back out the door, keys in hand.

It took a moment for Keith's eyes to adjust to the darkness. When they did, he realized the cop car he was looking at wasn't a cop car at all. It was a beat-up late-90s sedan with a matte black paint job and a single dashboard strobe. The strobe was the kind of light you could buy at a Spencer's Gifts.

Keith followed the bigger cop, Benny, to the back of the trailer. He could see that while the man did have the characteristic cop belt/ holster combo cinched around his waist, he *was* wearing black jeans. Up top, Benny was wearing what looked like the kind of plastic bag special button-down shirt that you'd buy at Marshall's. The shirt was baby blue instead of the NJPD's darker shade. The man wasn't wearing a hat and—from where Keith was standing—he couldn't even be sure if there was a badge anywhere on him. The cop's shirt didn't even have those little flaps on the shoulders.

Shit, Keith thought, realizing something about these two.

This area must have been so tax-cash poor and backwater that the county's police department couldn't afford proper uniforms. That was a sad state of affairs, even to Keith who hated cops. Maybe all those anti-Obama bumper stickers he'd seen out here were onto something.

They reached the U-Haul door and Benny turned, crossing his arms over his chest and looking bored. There was the glint of gold over his heart, a badge. Behind the beam, Flashlight Cop seemed to be similarly attired, but was himself wearing a pair of dark khakis. *Watch out, someone's dressing for the job they want and is on track to make Captain.*

"It's some real sick stuff back here. You're sure you want to see it?" Keith asked one last time, pretty confident he'd made his point by now.

"I am *so* sure," Flashlight Cop said. Beside him Benny stood sentinel, quiet but looming in his clip-on badge and black jeans.

Keith bent and unlocked the hatch, then lifted it up with solid metal clatter, the chain and pulley making the same sound a roller coaster made as it brought you up for your first drop. But there was also another sound over his shoulder, coming from where Benny was standing. It was a kind of click.

"Neato," the cop who'd done all the talking said.

Keith turned, putting his hand up to shield his eyes as he found the beam of the flashlight back in his face.

Blinded by the light, Keith Lumbra never saw what cracked him in the face, splitting his nose in two.

◆

Rory hit the man a second time, with a ferocity that, to his partner, registered as a killing blow.

"Be careful," Teeks warned, but not saying anything else as Rory scooped up the film director's unconscious body and laid him down roughly inside the trailer hitch. If the director slept for any length of time—balled up like that—he would have a hell of a sore neck. But maybe that was the least of his problems, considering the blood pouring from his nose.

Rory shuttered the trailer, took the keys from out of the lock, and wiped his baton off on his pant leg.

The bloodstain was invisible against the big man's black denim jeans.

Chapter One

"Silver or black?" Clarissa asked.

The kid stared back at her like she'd just asked him to find the square root of his parent's phone number.

"Should I sign in silver," she asked again, holding up silver the Sharpie to illustrate her point, "or black?"

"Whichever you think is best," the boy said.

She signed in silver, then paused before going back to fill in the inscription. "Should I make this out to you…"

God. Damn. It. The kid, maybe thirteen or fourteen, had said his name when he'd first walked up and shook her hand. But Clarissa could no longer remember the name after their silver or black Sharpie impasse had taken up so much brain power. It was the end of the weekend and she was tired, but still, this was frustrating. She *always* remembered names.

Of course the boy also had his hands pressed into his front pockets, one elbow obstructing the lanyard that might have sported a name tag, if she was lucky.

She'd made an oath when she'd first started doing these things: she would remember the fan's names, for at least as long as they were in front of her table. If she was charging twenty dollars for an autograph (a rate that had since gone up to thirty, in keeping with the market, but she would not lose the younger fans by charging forty), it was the least she could do. And, after all, the memorization wouldn't be difficult: she was a classically trained actor who'd started her career playing first Antigone and then Ophelia. That had been L.A. theater, not Broadway, but the work was still the work. Decades later she could still recall not only her lines, but most of her marks.

"It's Mark," the boy said. Then added with a nervous, between-clenched teeth laugh: "Yes, please personalize it. I'm not going to be putting this up on eBay or anything like that."

Maybe Clarissa couldn't remember their names because they all said the same things.

When she'd first started doing conventions, she would spend extra time with the young fans like Mark. They were the ones who had their moms and dads waiting for them the next aisle down, so as not to embarrass them in front of the talent. Clarissa used to find that cute.

But by now she'd heard the old "my older brother told me I had to watch *Death Birth*" and "I've got all your films on DVD. Even the out of print ones" stories enough to know that there was nothing special about younger fans. Particularly now that the internet had made everything she'd ever done readily available, even the movies Clarissa would have preferred to stay hidden.

"Is that with a 'C' or a 'K', Mark? I don't want to mess up a second time." She reached out like she was going to touch him, even though the span between them was comfortably two of her own arm's lengths. It was a body language trick she'd picked up, something to put the fans at ease.

She signed Mark-with-a-C's name, drew a tiny heart, then and sent him off with a smile and another moist handshake.

Clarissa would Purell later, but for now she sipped her bottled water and surveyed the line in front of her table. There were about fifteen people waiting, which was not a bad crowd for a Sunday.

Most of the fans in line now had either purchased a one-day only ticket to the convention (Sunday being the cheapest to attend) or had been saving meeting Clarissa Lee until they were sure there would be money left in their budgets.

She watched as her manager, Toby, took cash from an older man.

The fan wore thick glasses tethered to the back of his balding skull with one of those foam bands. The man was overweight, a round belly hanging over his shorts, and his t-shirt was speckled with what looked from Clarissa's vantage like the remnants of a sandwich.

Some stereotypes were cultural constructions meant to further rob power from the disenfranchised. And some stereotypes—as evidenced by the Urgeek standing in front of Clarissa's manager—were rooted in cold, unvarnished truth.

"Having her sign your own item is forty dollars per, and that price includes one picture with Ms. Lee," Toby said.

Without a pause, no deliberation as to whether he wanted to spend that much money, the Urgeek handed Toby a hundred dollar bill and with another twenty folded around it. He then turned to Clarissa.

He did not wait to receive any change.

The Urgeek's economy of movement told Clarissa that this was certainly not the man's first convention. In fact, it was very possible that she had signed for this guy last year and had already forgotten his face or blocked the memory out. There was a statute of limitations on *how long* she promised to remember their names.

The Urgeek clutched an envelope to his chest. If Clarissa were in a movie, there'd be an ominous close-up insert of that envelope.

"Hello Ms. Lee," the fan said, years of experience grinding his fake bashfulness down to an autistic's monotone. *There's still time for you to grow out of it, Marc,* she thought, thinking back to the teenager. It was something to amuse herself while the guy laid the envelope on the table and fanned out the three glossy photographs he'd brought with him.

"Could you sign all three of these 'To Kurt, with love'? Please?"

Before her, there were three faces, all pouting and all hers, six breasts, all raised with a twenty-seven year old's indigence to gravity, and—in one picture—a dark wisp of pubis. Clarissa Lee's *Playboy* spread, dating from the era where she'd first realized that film work might not keep coming in forever, was the gift that kept on giving.

She did not clarify the spelling of his name, but she did sign Kurt's photos "with love" and then took a picture with him, Toby squeezing himself out from behind the table to point Kurt's digital camera.

"You still look great," Kurt whispered to her in the second before the flash. His breath was a fetid version of the pepperoni and bread stink that hangs on your clothes for a few minutes after visiting a Subway restaurant.

Tired as she was, as much as she wanted the weekend to be over, Clarissa Lee did not break character. "Aw. Thank you," she said, shooing him away with her eyes. Their transaction was finished. She did not regret the photoshoot, but it was interactions like this one that brought her damn close to it.

The next fan in line looked like a spritz of fresh air. She was a girl in her late twenties or early thirties, buttons polka-dotting her hooded sweatshirt and messenger bag. In short: your classic "geek girl" type. She bought a single 8x10 for thirty dollars from Toby and then set down a small Tupperware container in front of Clarissa.

The girl was adorable, but that Tupperware was worrisome.

Clarissa asked her name with a manic quality that she hadn't meant to creep into her voice.

Oh Christ. Please don't let that be—

"I'm Sephera, and I hope you don't think this is awkward or weird or anything, but I brought you a birthday cake."

Sephera opened the Tupperware to reveal a single cupcake. And there was the reminder, written in red gelatin icing meant to look like blood:

Today, Clarissa Lee was fifty-five years old.

Chapter Two

It was possible that most conventioneers, because they attended the same cons every year and found the vendor rooms mostly unchanged, had no idea how quickly a hotel ballroom can be emptied. Subconsciously, there were probably many fans who thought the con stayed there year round. Like how Disneyland continued to exist even when you weren't riding the Matterhorn Bobsleds.

But as soon as the last attendee was scooted out the door by volunteer security, the tables and booths started disappearing. Wing-nuts were spun from collapsible signage, racks of grey market t-shirts (Clarissa certainly never saw any residuals from her likeness being sold two-for-twenty) were emptied into plastic containers, and black tablecloths were folded up.

The convention was boxed and loaded into a fleet of trucks, vans, and the occasional hearse with the trained precision of a circus leaving town after the last of the rubes had been bilked. The fans themselves might linger in the hotel bar or hit the con suite for a dead-dog party, but the people for whom this was a business and nothing more? At five o'clock on Sunday it was time for them to jet.

Clarissa and Toby didn't have much to pack and their plane back to L.A. wasn't until eight fifteen, so there was time. She stood and watched the room around her be dismantled.

She could relax because there wasn't much to pack. Well, there wasn't much for *Clarissa* to pack. Toby would take care of it all, the vinyl banner that clipped onto the edge of the table and the stacks of 8x10s that had to be loaded back into their printer-paper boxes.

On the other side of the aisle from her, she watched the awkward post-mating rituals of two celebrities who had the look about them like they'd gotten drunk and dirty the night before. She wasn't close enough to hear what they were saying to each other but she could read the body language.

The guy, an out of work bit player and still-working porno actor named Ivan Butinelli was trying to help a visibly hungover Gina Bright pack up her table. Even without hearing what they were saying, the interaction was painfully awkward. Clarissa couldn't look away.

Bright was a slightly younger Clarissa Lee knock-off, if Clarissa were petty enough to put a label on it, which she wasn't. Not one bit.

Clarissa doubted that Butinelli had a wife at home, but she wondered if Bright's red-cheeks were due to some kind of shame or if they were always that red, these days.

Despite both of the other celebrities being familiar faces on the con circuit, Clarissa wouldn't have been able to place their names if she ran into them on the street. No, all weekend she'd had no choice but to stare across at their banners whenever business got slow at her own table. They were people she saw every few months, but watching them from afar, like an anthropological study. She always forgot to take notes.

Breaking Clarissa from her voyeurist's soap opera, Toby hefted the cashbox onto the table in front of her with a clatter. He then began to transfer Sunday's take, a fat stack of bills, from the zippered envelope he'd been using to make change. He then locked the cashbox and handed the key to Clarissa.

Giving her the key for safekeeping was unnecessary. Clarissa trusted Toby implicitly, but part of that trust stemmed from the fact that he was nervous to a fault. In fact, Toby was so concerned with not

being seen as a cheat that it often worked against his ability to manage
her career effectively, in some ways making him worse than if he were
both successful and cheating her.

"How'd we do?" she asked. By virtue of her line only flagging
once or twice all weekend, she assumed they'd done okay.

"Better than fair, I'd say." Toby said, stacking photos, placing a
page of acid-free paper between each variety so they were easier to
unpack. The way he zoned in to focus on his work could have been
exhaustion from the weekend or could have been him softening the
blow of a lackluster con. It was hard to tell with Toby. He was a bad liar
but also fidgety as hell when telling the truth.

At cons Clarissa offered fifteen varieties of glossy photo. Two
of them were miniature posters of her two most well known films.
One was 1979's *Night Visitor*, her first starring role and a mildly
violent whodunit that had been in production around the same time
as *Halloween*'s release. After Carpenter's success and the first wave of
imitators the film had gone back to Canada for gory reshoots and a star
was born. The other was 1988's *Death Birth*, a critical and commercial
flop that had recently grown a rabid fanbase because of the director's
later big-budget studio work.

That director was Boyd Haight and Clarissa should have never
married him.

Or never have divorced him. At the very least she should not have
pushed for separation when she did, when she had been the one who'd
taken the hit in court. Now "once married to Boyd Haight" was the top
piece of trivia on her IMDB and Wikipedia pages, no matter how many
times she tried to log in and edit them. In 1991 it would have been the
other way around. He would have been 'the ex-husband' instead of her
being 'the ex-wife.' Had either of those websites existed back then.

Many mistakes had been made, financial and personal. But Toby
kept her in enough work, much of it voiceover, that she could pay rent.

The rest of the 8x10s were various headshots and production stills, the most recent of which was fifteen years old and featured Clarissa with foam latex ridges on her chin, a prosthesis that she wore to play an alien in a recurring part on a basic cable sci-fi show.

The *Nebula Journey* headshot didn't move many units at a show like this weekend's, but when she did sell one she knew to stay alert for the unanswerable continuity questions that were probably headed her way. The horror nerds asked her which international cuts of her films she preferred and the sci-fi nerds asked about FTL drives and the mating rituals of her character's alien species.

A few minutes later in the process of packing, Toby needed help wrestling a bungee cord around the vinyl banner. Ten minutes after that their bags were out of the coat check and placed into a cab.

Sitting quietly while Toby messed with his phone, Clarissa watched the combination hotel and convention center recede into the distance.

The sensation was like leaving a summer camp that you never much enjoyed, where even the friends you made weren't really friends and you could never get the hang of sleeping through the night in your bunk. But there was still that pang of regret, wanting to say goodbye to a temporary home. There was also, Clarissa had to admit, something nice about spending a weekend being worshipped and desired. It beat most other work.

Seeing the post-coital odd couple that was Ivan Butinelli and Gina Bright reminded Clarissa that she herself had only ever gotten lucky once at one of these things. And that once had been *lucky* enough.

Her reluctance to hook up wasn't just that old chestnut about mistakenly mixing business with pleasure, but also because there were slim pickings at these cons. Handsome as they could be, shacking up with a B-level actor would have been something she regretted, and she'd made enough similar mistakes during her TV years. With the convention's guest list out of the equation, that only left vendors and attendees in the prospect pool.

In terms of physique, men at these conventions were either perennial teenage string beans or guys who would do *anything* short of eat actual vegetation to be considered string beans. Neither did much for her, hence her celibacy.

For her lone sexual conquest, Clarissa had chosen to avoid all three sub-classifications of con life entirely.

It happened at New Jersey's Chiller Theatre in 2008, an east coast convention easy to attend for both its proximity to JFK and the fact that Toby could schedule whatever New York meetings he could muster during the same week. Her and this guy, they'd met at the hotel bar and judging from his button-down shirt, stubble-less cheeks, and dress pants, he wasn't a horror fan and was staying at the hotel on unrelated business. They didn't spend their brief courtship talking about what they did for a living and if he'd recognized her at all then he'd been playing it like he didn't.

Their affair had been brief but successful, twice successful. But, lying in bed, he'd ruined the afterglow by saying he was at the con looking for investors for a project that she'd be great in. Insult to injury, he wanted to cast her as the grown protagonist's mother.

Clarissa gathered her clothes and advised the guy to make sure to fuck Dee Wallace next time.

"Isn't it a flat rate?" Toby said in a whine to the driver, his wrists resting against the cab's partition. He was arguing with the cabbie about the meter.

"No sir. I didn't pick you up downtown. I'm sorry, I had to run the meter."

Toby, not much of a fighter, just shrugged and paid the man. He included a twenty percent tip, seemingly oblivious to the fact that he'd just voiced suspicions about being fleeced.

They entered the terminal, Toby grunting when he had to lift her rolling bag over the curb.

In the harsh light of the United ticketing area, Toby looked even more nervous than he had when stacking up 8x10s. Was it something he'd read on his phone that had soured his mood? Had she whiffed an audition? Was Clarissa being squeezed out of residuals? At this point in the day she didn't much care, she just wanted to get back to her apartment, to her cat, to a city where most people weren't familiar with the phrase "packing lip."

Toby approached one of the automated check-in machines, swiped his debit card, and swore as no boarding passes materialized.

Over his shoulder Clarissa could read the words "See Desk" on the screen. There was no please, no thank you, just "See Desk."

Instead of starting towards the line to speak with a representative, Toby turned to Clarissa and asked: "Can I have the key please?"

It took her a moment to figure out which key he meant.

"My card was declined, I need to pay for our tickets with cash," he said.

Clarissa squinted at him, feeling her face begin to flush in an embarrassment that her conscious mind hadn't quite settled into yet.

"How about I just use my credit—"

"No, your accounts aren't in the greatest shape, it would be best if we just used the cashbox instead of a card."

Clarissa handed over the key, watched him count out a few hundred dollars in cash, and girded herself to have a terribly awkward in-flight conversation.

She'd been told by several different people that having all-in-one representation had been a bad idea, a manager-slash-agent-slash-accountant, but the warnings never hit home until that moment.

Chapter Three

"If you don't know Kane Hodder's email or phone number then what the fuck are you good for?" Rory asked as he dipped low, brandishing the pliers.

The kid tied to the chair was running low on finger nails. Rory pulled another one off.

As soon as he was done screaming, he spoke: "I'm not! I'm not even related to him in…in…in," he started to fade again, a broken record with a glistening string of spit now connecting his chin to his t-shirt.

Rory had heard the excuse so many times by now he was starting to believe it. "But I'm not his assistant," the kid had sputtered, back when he'd been able to string together full sentences. Before the broken teeth and Rory's pliers. "I was a volunteer at the con, I hadn't even met him until Friday! I just got him water and made sure that his line was wrapping around the table like it was supposed to be!"

Not Hodder's assistant? No, Rory guessed that made sense. Why would Jason Voorhees fly his own people out to the middle of nowhere? The man could handle himself, Rory was sure.

"You get your shirt," Rory said and pointed down to where it read 'Staff' over the kid's heart, "and you start to think that you're better than everyone else. Well, I've got this and I know that that ain't true: Jonathan Benson from *Ohio*." He read it O-Hi-O, really dragging it out.

Rory had taken the kid's license out of his wallet, along with forty bucks in cash and a Cheesecake Factory gift card for an undisclosed amount. Cheesecake Factory? Fancy. This fucking hick kid was used to putting on airs, Rory was sure of it.

"You aren't from Hollywood, Johnny," Rory said. "So the way I see it: you brought this on yourself for acting like it. All we wanted from you was some *information*."

"*We?*" Jonathan asked, the word more of a whimper, the squeaky release of air from a balloon, than it was a real question.

That was right, Teeks wasn't in the room with Rory. In fact, Teeks wasn't aware of the snatch-up of Jonathan Benson at all. Boy, would Teeks be angry if he found out that Rory was striking out on his own. Even if he was just trying to help, he wanted to make Teeks some more 'connections'.

"Never you mind *we*, Jonathan. Never you mind," Rory said, trying to channel his best TV investigator, the tall guy who beat up all those pedos on *Law & Order*. That guy was tall—way taller than Kane Hodder, it turned out—but Rory was taller and more jacked than both of them. "I'm gonna ask you one last time: you don't have contact info for Mr. Hodder?"

Johnny Benson didn't speak, just nodded and mumbled like someone talking in their sleep.

Rory took the blade from his boot, clapped a big hand over Johnny's mouth, and ran the knife over the boy's throat.

It was only once the blood had gone everywhere that Rory panicked, realizing he'd have to get all of this cleaned up before Teeks called or came over looking for him.

An unsanctioned kidnapping?

Stupid stupid stupid, Rory. How are we going to succeed like this?

Chapter Four

To understand how things could get so fucked, to understand how Clarissa Lee couldn't see the end of the drop coming until it was too late, one needed to understand one industry term: pay-or-play contracts.

Not to be confused with the music industry's pay-*to*-play or conscription model, pay-or-play is an agreement that sees on-screen talent getting paid *even if* the movie in question never ends up getting made.

These kinds of deals weren't typical in the world of straight-to-video—or now straight-to-Netflix—productions Clarissa had found herself working recently. But it wasn't impossible that investors who put money into a C-level horror movie would also insist on at least one name fans would recognize. And it was just a small jump in logic from that proven trend to the idea that a "star cameo" player might be able to insist on money up front, not upon completion.

When the money had stopped coming in several years ago, Toby, in a bout of delusional protectiveness, had made a big mistake. He decided that the best course of action was to tell Clarissa she'd booked several pay-or-play deals that didn't actually exist. That way, when the fake movies fell apart she wouldn't be suspicious as to how she could still be paying her bills.

This information took a silent half hour of waiting for departure and then forty-five minutes of questioning to acquire. Once they were surrounded by the white noise of the plane's engines and were able to recline their seats, Toby gave up the goods. After he'd admitted that yes all the work was gone and now the money was too, he started crying. Instead of keeping her seat and trying to console him, Clarissa took her three miniature bottles of Kettle One into the bathroom and sat for a long time.

A little drunk and looking to spend money as a 'fuck you' to Toby, Clarissa purchased the use of the in-flight wifi. Her bank card wasn't declined, so she now either had a $14.95 overdraft or there was *some* gas left in the tank.

After boredom set in scanning through the same six stories—these days *Deadline*, *Variety*, and the fan blogs offered very little editorializing on the press releases they were sent from the studios—Clarissa decided that she would try and check her email accounts.

She hadn't logged into them in a while, that was part of Toby's job description. Her public account, for which there was a form on her website, was a mess of mildly-concerning fan letters and penis pill spam. Her business email would be where the action was.

Toby had set up both accounts but, with the same transparency with which he had dealt with the cashbox key, he wanted Clarissa to be able to access them. The passwords weren't difficult to remember.

This professional account (clarissalee.tobygivens@gmail.com) was only accessible either through direct contact with Toby, various casting director's rolodexes, or through IMDB's paid Pro accounts. Besides his name and a high-gloss picture of Clarissa, the email was the only information on Toby's business card.

Someone knocked on the bathroom door.

"Occupied!" Clarissa yelled and then frowned into the glow of her phone screen. Why couldn't Toby have just named the account clarissalee.manager@gmail.com?

Once she fired Toby she was going to have to start a new account and migrate over all her contacts.

She was going to have to change a lot of things.

No. No thinking about that. There had to be some kind of job in here she could do for quick cash with minimal debasement.

◆

Dear Ms. Lee (or associated representation),

I hope that this letter finds you well. My associates and I at **MTY Productions** are huge fans and would like to extend the invitation for you to be Guest of Honor at our inaugural convention.

Now, I am well aware that there are other conventions competing for your time and energy, but please allow me a moment to explain why **Blood Camp Con** is worthy of your attention.

With the enthusiastic support of our creative partners (which include Keith Lumbra of **Rigor Mortis Films**, a leading name in extreme horror) and financial backers, we believe we have created the world's most immersive fan experience.

Structured more like a summer camp than a comic convention, **Blood Camp Con** attendees will spend the weekend living in a horror film. If that sounds off-putting, please understand that as a guest you will be living those three days in complete comfort, only required to participate in a few role-playing exercises on par in strenuousness with a walk-on cameo in a film.

We are a boutique convention, and as such our business model has to be structured a little differently from the HorrorHounds and Weekend of Horrors of the world. The convention will not only supply you room and board for the weekend, but we will also pay your airfare and provide ground transportation.

Since you will not be charging for autographs and photo-ops, you and the rest of the guests will be provided a royalty share based on ticket sales.

To keep the con intimate, attendance will be capped at a hundred attendees, but don't worry that won't mean less profit for you. With **Premiere Deluxe** packages that cap in price at $8,000 and many tickets already pre-sold before the guest list has been announced: I feel confident to guarantee you will earn at least ten-thousand dollars. Possibly much more.

And of course half of that guarantee (**$5,000**) can be sent as an **advance** in good faith.

Please reply as soon as possible so we do not have to pursue another, lesser, Guest of Honor. The dates of the event are October 15th-17th and you would be flying into Cincinnati's CVG.

On a personal note, whether or not you take us up on our offer or even respond to this email, I'd like to say that your work has changed my life.

Warmest Wishes,
Michael Teeks

♦

She read most of that email, but wasn't quite sure it was saying much of anything about what the event actually was. Or maybe it was the booze.

With the third miniature bottle of vodka inside her—well, mostly, some had dribbled down her chin—Clarissa struggled to thumb out a reply.

Halfway through she was interrupted by another knock. She shushed whoever was knocking at the bathroom door, and continued typing her message.

**Michael, Sounds great send the money and I'll see you in
octopus.**

Clarissa did not catch her phone's autocorrect for October.

After hitting 'send' she opened the door to find a flight attendant
hunched over. She had been listening at the folding door's seam, and
ready to knock again when Clarissa had surprised her.

"I'm fine," Clarissa said to the woman, a little too loud and her
face hovering a little too close to the flight attendant's. Clarissa wasn't
much of a drinker, and the invisible alcohol vapor trails she could feel
curling from her mouth and nostrils as she spoke surprised her, made
her feel like a drunk dragon.

She returned to her seat, holding onto the seatbacks to fight her
own internal turbulence as she navigated the aisle.

Slipping into the seat beside Toby, Clarissa gave an unladylike
yelp as the cool metal of her seatbelt buckle touched the skin above her
underwear and below the end of her shirt.

"Don't say anything, just know that I have paid for the wifi so you
can spend the rest of the flight sending emails and trying to get yourself
unfired," she said and handed her phone to Toby.

He had the wet eyes and quivering chin of a whipped dog, but he
followed her instructions and unlocked her iPhone with a click.

Clarissa then promptly fell asleep, and upon arriving in L.A. she
had forgotten all about the email she'd sent to Michael Teeks.

Chapter Five

Teeks looked up from his laptop to see Rory's bare ass in front of him. The curls of Rory's crack-hair had been pressed into a series of butterfly wings against either butt cheek.

It was not a pretty sight.

"What are you changing in here for?" Teeks asked, averting his eyes but still watching Rory hop into the legs of the pants in his peripheral vision, a gimp ballerina.

"I gotta watch him, don't I?" Rory said, tossing his head to indicate the director sitting on the couch.

Teeks was set up at the kitchen table, his laptop and phone out in front of him, a ledger of graph paper beside those.

"Well. A: I'm here to watch him. And, B: you didn't need to take off your underwear to try it on, did you?"

"I guess not," Rory said. The big man tried to pull up both the pants and his tighty-whities simultaneously and failed, one thumb becoming unhooked and the elastic snapping. The giant man-child smiled some more at that. Rory was capable of great gaiety and great violence, sometimes within the same moment.

Keith Lumbra sat and stared at his hands. The director was not laughing, but at least he'd stopped sweating and trembling. They had connected Keith's ankles using two zipties, leaving his hands free to work. If the plastic ties weren't enough of an impediment, his left eye had swollen almost completely shut and when he exhaled through his nose the wind whistled out of three holes instead of two.

Teeks had to hand it to Lumbra, though: once Teeks had explained what they needed done, the director had been very amenable and worked well under pressure.

The design process for Rory's costume had started with a brainstorming session, Rory enthusiastically throwing out choices and even providing some sketches for what he wanted it to look like.

The problem with Rory, outside of his limited artistic skills, was that he lacked any sense of originality. All of his ideas were slight variations on stuff that had been done before. For example:

"A football helmet, with barbwire wrapped around the face guard," Rory said. *A sports mask, really?*

"I want long black streamers on my arms, almost like wings." Teeks couldn't tell if Rory was ripping off *Scream* or *Batman* with that one. Or which was more embarrassing as a self-respecting horror fan.

"A pig head that's also a hat, so that I have two sets of eyes!" Teeks didn't remember where he'd heard that exact one before, but he nixed the idea based on the *Motel Hell* associations alone.

Teeks had said he'd take all of Rory's suggestions under advisement. He didn't really, though. He'd used his design and Photoshop skills to whip up something that was, in his opinion, rather original. Teeks' design wouldn't rely on no off-the-rack mask, no jumpsuit, no Farmer John shit. No: their slasher would be modern. Truly Satanic. A beast straight from hell.

Teeks watched Rory try on the jacket, struggling to get the zipper started. Even from the back the metal studs and protruding bones looked cool. They would look even better at night, with the right accent lighting.

"It fits?" Teeks asked and in response Rory lifted his arms above his head and flexed. There was the sound of stretched leather and canvas, but all of the jacket's FX alterations stayed put. Nothing dropped off or broke. Keith Lumbra may have turned into a real baby while begging for his life, but the man could stitch a seam and cast a latex mold with the best of them, even under duress.

"Let me try on the mask, just for a second," Rory asked, not looking to the mask's creator, but instead posing his question to Teeks.

Teeks looked to Lumbra on the couch, who just shrugged. "No," Teeks said, "He's not finished with it yet. You'll end up breaking it."

"Damn it!" Rory said, turning to address their captive collaborator now. "You best remember who gave you that." Rory pointed at the crusty gauze taped over Lumbra's nose. He could have meant the broken nose or the travel first aid kit that Lumbra had been allowed to use to try and patch up the trauma on his own. A skilled costume craftsman Lumbra may have been, but a doctor he clearly was not.

Teeks' email notification chimed and he tabbed over to check the message. It was a response to one of his guest of honor inquiries.

He read the short email twice, feeling his mood improve each time through the short message.

"Oh what the hell? Try on the mask, but be careful with the damn thing. We've got ourselves a star now."

Chapter Six

There was no escaping it: these people secretly ruled the world.

Marcus Lang wasn't technically in the same city as the convention. He was up the highway a couple of exits. Even that far from the vendors' hall, he was looking at two supermarket aisles stocked with plastic skulls, bloody window decals, and vinyl costume smocks that turned your kids into zombies, complete with unspooling intestines.

It was September 2nd and the convention had followed him out onto the byways of New Jersey.

To listen to horror fans talk about their interests, they made themselves out to be the wounded minority, a niche market that was never fully taken seriously by content creators and ostracized by the culture at large. But looking at the aisle of Halloween decorations in front of him, that us vs. them act didn't hold much water. America loved this shit. At this point they dedicated one-sixth of the year to it.

It was Friday night and Marcus had taken his rental car out for a spin, always eager to check out what new and exotic chain-stores the different regions of the country had to offer. Ludicrously early Halloween aisle aside, Wegmans was a pleasant supermarket to walk around.

After-hours, most of his peers either went up to their hotel rooms or hung out around the convention, either in the bar or at the official meet-and-greet costume party. Unless Marcus was getting paid, he didn't spend any more time with horror-people than he had to. It's not that he didn't like them, quite the contrary: his fans could be sweet and kind.

But as a black man who'd grown up in a Baptist home, he was uncomfortable—on a lot of levels—around white guys with face and neck tattoos. He couldn't help it.

So he used these trips as opportunities to explore the strip-malls and supermarkets of suburban America. Boring? Maybe. Enjoyable? *Completely and utterly.*

Marcus pushed his cart around.

Occasionally he would pick up an item, consider buying it, only to remember that his motel room had no way to prepare whatever it was he wanted. The Wegmans had a nice bakery section, though, and he'd picked up a tray of muffins. Whatever he didn't eat tonight he could share with his table neighbors tomorrow morning.

Fans loved to see that kind of thing, watching two celebrities interact. *I knew they had to be friends in real life!* You could hear them squeal, safe with the knowledge that this was just a confirmation of what they'd already hoped and halfway believed.

Wait, did he just mentally refer to himself as the c-word? *Shit.*

Celebrities drove fancy cars, had people to answer the phone, and couldn't walk around a Wegmans without being hassled. Marcus Lang was not a celebrity.

Signing glossy pictures of yourself all day had a way of changing your self-image, inflating and skewing your successes. At a con, anytime he went to the bathroom there was a weird sense of time-traveling if he caught his reflection in the mirror. It was like: *oh yeah,* Marcus Lang got old since appearing in *Guardians of Hell.* For the last decade he'd been keeping his head shaved, and his mustache was now more grey than black.

He tried not to think about it and moved on from the bakery case and inspected the different flavors of Greek yogurt on offering in the dairy section. He frowned again when he saw that there was a new, seasonal flavor on offering.

Pumpkin yogurt? The Halloween crowd were now masters of the fucking universe.

"Excuse me, Mr. Lang?" a voice called from behind him.

Speak of the devil, maybe he *was* a celebrity. Marcus put the yogurt back on the rack, taking a half-second to mentally prepare himself before turning around.

Instead of a kid with a black t-shirt, scraggly beard, and a wallet chain (it may sound specific, but there were *so* many wallet chains at these things), Marcus was surprised to find a middle-aged man, looking that age in dress pants and a sports coat. The guy had recently shaved and his teeth were white and symmetrical behind his smile. He had his hand out to Marcus.

Marcus's first thought was: *Hollywood*. The surreal nature of seeing this L.A. man standing in the fluorescent lighting of a New Jersey supermarket was almost too much to square, but Marcus took the offered hand and shook it.

"This may sound a little creepy," the guy said. "I had tried to call to you in the lobby but you must not have heard me, I followed you outside, and by the time I'd almost caught up you were in your car and I was near mine and well. Here we are."

No, not all the way Hollywood. There was an accent there being suppressed, but from where Marcus couldn't tell.

"You've been following me since the hotel?" Marcus asked.

The man laughed. "As long as you don't call it 'stalking'" he said, sounding embarrassed by the whole exchange but also with an immoderate amount of confidence. It was like: yes, he knew how he looked, knew how he was dressed, and knew that the combination of those things wasn't going to get him slapped with a restraining order or even a polite brush-off. The guy was so smooth, he must've taken lessons, maybe even taught a class or two on the subject.

"Marcus," the guy said, giving the briefest of pauses for a *Can I call you Marcus?* to exist in the ellipsis, "My name's Michael Teeks and I wanted to talk to you because your people haven't been responding to my emails."

He had to try not to laugh at that. Marcus didn't have people. He had email.

Marcus made a comfortable living but that was more luck than anything his former agent had done for him. Betsy Kline had gotten him bit parts in nearly fifty movies from 1982-1994. One day, during an especially dismal phone call looking for more substantial work, she'd delivered upon him the no-prize title of the "handsomest character actor in history." But, it turned out, a handful of those bit parts had been the equivalent of buying penny stocks and having them grow into Microsoft or Starbucks. Never mind the residuals: Marcus Lang was a cult figure and could now support himself with very little effort. And very little traditional acting work. No agent needed.

"And what emails were those, Mr. Teeks?"

Teeks didn't correct Marcus with a *Michael, please* before continuing. "Our convention, Blood Camp Con, we sent an invite and then a stinger email."

Marcus *had* read those emails. To him, the three thousand dollar advance the organizers were promising sounded ridiculous. He'd received similar offers before, profit-share schemes from indie filmmakers who didn't know the first thing about the business, startup conventions like this one that offered signing bonuses and then dissolved and cancelled the event before the checks could be cashed.

Neverminding all that, the professionalism red flags had gone off when Mr. Teeks had wanted to put on a convention that didn't even list a location or hotel in the email. Or a state, even. Marcus had looked up the airport code CVG. It was used for Cincinnati, but the airport itself was technically located across the border in Northern Kentucky.

Instead of getting caught in a lie, Marcus scrunched his face into what he hoped was a mix of confusion and interest while allowing Teeks to continue talking. He could tell from the guy's posture and sudden intake of breath that he was about to get an elevator pitch.

"We're creating an immersive experience, trying to tap into the hardcore market in a way that most conventions can't do anymore. *The Walking Dead* is the most popular show on television. This shit isn't niche anymore and the old-school fans, the ones with disposable income, are looking for something different."

"True, true," Marcus said, nodding his head. His back and ass were starting to get chilly from the cool wafting off the dairy cabinet.

"In the email I had talked about a three thousand dollar advance. What if I made it four?"

"And what would I have to do? If I'm not going to be signing and taking pictures," Marcus said, the words coming out before he thought them through.

Fuck. Teeks hadn't said anything about not charging for autographs and photo ops, he was remembering that detail from the email he'd ignored. Twice.

Teeks gave a tiny shark smile, but didn't look distressed. "Consider it more like a role in a film than attending a convention. You'll be asked to act briefly. Only there's no way for things to get fucked up and be called back for reshoots," Teeks laughed like he'd made a joke with several layers. There was only one that Marcus could parse: that the guy wanted to look and sound like a showbiz insider. "To be quite honest, Marcus: we've already got our star guest lined-up. Anyone else would just be…"

Marcus bristled, he didn't mean to but he did, perhaps it was the freeze falling off the refrigerated yogurt shelf. Teeks caught this change in attitude.

"All we need now is some cannon fodder," Teeks said. "What do you say?"

Chapter Seven

An overdose of nervous energy worked miracles for Toby Givens. Clarissa should have been threatening to fire him every six months for the length of her career, the same way that it was good to periodically clear out your temporary internet files so your computer didn't slow down.

Back in May, after she'd returned from the bathroom, he'd used the expensive plane wifi to secure her gigs. Then after they'd landed, using more small bills from the cashbox to pay the taxi, Clarissa didn't get a full eight hours of sleep before being awoken by phone call from Toby that he had booked her even more work.

Where was this fire when she was slowly going broke?

In the days after learning that he'd been scamming her—a soft-hearted scam, but a scam—it occurred to Clarissa that Toby could have just as easily been lying about this new work. Even once she saw that cash was coming in, there was no way of telling that Toby wasn't putting all his personal belongings up on Craigslist and eBay in order to get the money. Then she realized that she didn't much care. He'd lied about how she'd hit poverty row, he could lie about how she was working her way back to solvency, as long as the money was green.

Toby's hustle was admirable and never much flagged in the three months it took to receive a reminder about Blood Camp Con. The convention that—oh yeah—Clarissa had signed herself up for on the flight. It may have been after three vodkas, but her agreement was still legally binding. Probably.

"They want to know where to send the check," Toby said, fixing his glasses the way he did when he was anxious or annoyed, one of his many fidgety tells. "Did you do any research into these guys at all?"

"You mean on the plane? Before or after I was told that you'd lost my life savings? No, I must not have been thinking."

Toby scrunched up his face, making his man-baby features even more prominent.

"Give them an address. If they send us five grand and the check doesn't bounce, we go and do it. Can't be any worse than signing at the pro wrestling convention," Clarissa said.

As part of a more "aggressive" convention presence, Toby had extended their touring to include smaller shows and ancillary markets that had the potential for 'fanbase spillover.'

"That wrestling thing was an honest mistake," Toby said.

"It was at an Elks Lodge!"

That ended the argument. Toby told them where to send the advance and a week later Clarissa was endorsing a check from MTY Productions for five thousand dollars.

Two months later they were landing, a flight attendant welcoming them to Hebron, Kentucky.

"Kentucky?" Clarissa asked, shortly after touchdown.

Cincinnati's airport wasn't in Ohio, which was news to Clarissa but didn't seem to surprise Toby.

"Northern Kentucky, but Cincinnati is right over the bridge on the other side of the river. Don't you remember geography class?" Toby asked. He'd been her only representation and one of her only friends for fifteen years and still Toby was full of geeky, sobering surprises. His knowledge pool was as vast and deep as it was useless.

"Geography class? Do schools even offer that, or was it some kind of club you belonged to?" Clarissa said, walking up the air gate towards the terminal. "I didn't even know Ohio bordered fucking Kentucky."

This last part drew angry stares from the people in front of and behind them. A mother with a child at her hip dragging a rolling suitcase muttered "real nice" under her breath.

That was right. Some of these people *lived* in Kentucky.

Clarissa and Toby worked their way past the gate kiosks, following signs for ground transportation. The entire time Toby stared into his phone, occasionally tripped up by the sudden appearance or disappearance of moving walkways.

"Where are we headed?" Clarissa asked. They had no checked baggage, which was a nice change of pace. No reason to check baggage when they didn't need to bring her banner or 8x10s.

"The email said that we would be met at the—"

"Nevermind," Clarissa said, pointing to the bottom of the escalator where a young woman held out a handwritten sign reading: "Ms. Lee".

Clarissa watched the metal stairs feed into the teeth ahead of them. When riding escalators she was constantly aware of the machinery underfoot. At least she'd been vigilant ever since she was once killed by one in a film.

Looking up after stepping up, Clarissa could see that their chauffeur was not just a young woman but a *very* young woman. Young enough that she may not have been their chauffeur. It was possible that she wasn't old enough to drive.

As Clarissa wheeled her suitcase off the last step, the girl began to wave. The girl watched Clarissa approach, the corners of her mouth ending in two dimples, each one deep enough to swallow a Buick. She had straight dirty blonde hair pulled back in a simple ponytail. Her face wasn't plain, but it was a face that could have benefited from some light makeup.

"We see you," Clarissa said to her, not trying to be rude, but finding herself a little embarrassed to have such an eager welcoming party.

Toby followed, the three of them forming a tight triangle that everyone disembarking the escalator had to maneuver around.

"Welcome to Kentucky, Ms. Lee," the young girl said, her voice high and young, matching her face and stature. The voice was not only sweet and chipper, it was without trace of an accent, at least none that Clarissa could pick up on.

Clarissa Lee *hadn't* come to Hollywood on a Trailways bus with nothing but a hatbox full of dreams. She *didn't* start out as a drop-dead gorgeous but down-on-her-luck waitress discovered by a studio head.

No, Clarissa Lee had been raised in Pasadena, and had known from a young age that she would be entering the industry when she finished high school. If she kept her grades up, maybe auditioning for commercial work before then.

Her "left coast" life notwithstanding, she knew on a theoretical level that she should not prejudge anyone from the middle of the country. Having starred in enough movies where Griffith Park had doubled for Appalachia, she didn't fear the country like a city girl should. She knew that the killer redneck was a Hollywood construction. But still, she had expected the person who picked them up to at least have an accent.

"Y'all have any other luggage?" The girl asked. Ah, there it was: *y'all*. Prejudice balance restored.

"No, this is it," Toby said, the girl looking in his direction for the first time. Toby put his hand out. "Toby Givens. I'm Ms. Lee's manager."

The girl hesitated a moment, her mind doing some kind of calculation, allowing for a variable, then she shook his hand. "Kimberly Yost. I'm one of the Production Assistants for the Con."

That was interesting, calling the convention volunteers P.A.s. Clarissa had never encountered that before.

Although Kim was wearing a camp counselor's baseball t-shirt and "retro" shorts that rode high on her stomach and short on her ass, Clarissa could tell that she was normally one of those black t-shirted goth girls. The kind of girls who wore chokers instead of necklaces and tortured their hair with cheap, off-beat dye jobs. Kimberly was in need of a little girlish guidance if she was going to present herself as appropriately professional, but Clarissa wasn't going to end up being the mentor to give it to her. She decided that much right now.

"It's very nice to meet you, Kim. Do you think we can go to the car now?" Clarissa asked, taking a glance up at the annoyed faces leaving the escalator they were blocking.

Kimberly's eyes fuzzed and her megawatt smile flickered, but only for a moment.

"Oh, of course. Mr. Teeks wanted me to make sure all your baggage was accounted for, to introduce myself, and then to bring you out to campus," Kim said, mostly to herself it seemed. It was like she was going back over a mental list. The girl didn't strike Clarissa as dumb, but she was carrying that 'first day on the job' shellshock that Clarissa had seen hundreds of times on the faces of similar kids. There were worse ways these nerves could have manifested themselves. At least Kimberly was talking and smiling, not shutting down. Clarissa tried to remember *ever* caring that much about a job. She knew that if Kimberly continued in this business long enough—and in the entertainment hotbed of Kentucky how couldn't she?—that enthusiasm would be drummed out of her. Likely with great haste.

Kimberly's disillusionment could begin on the ride to "campus," wherever the fuck that was. Who knew if Clarissa, fabulous Hollywood movie star, would live up to the standard that Kim had already built in her mind? Clarissa Lee caught herself saying or thinking something jaded on a daily basis, but most days she reminded herself that she wasn't "jaded," just experienced.

Clarissa thought of the pain in her lower-back, how grumpy air travel made her for most of the day, and calculated that it wouldn't be long until she said or did something unpleasant to Kim. She would try her best not to, though.

"You lead the way, Kim!" Clarissa smiled, allowing the girl to take the handle of her suitcase from Toby as she skipped—literally skipped—away toward arrivals parking.

They reached the loading and unloading zone and Kim asked them to wait while she disappeared into a nearby lot, speedwalking.

"She seems eager," Clarissa said. Toby looked up from his phone.

"Yes. Very. Sorry, I'm just going back and forth on this," Toby said, indicating a chain of emails. There were things that Toby got himself very worked up about that ended up having *very* little influence on his own life and even less impact on Clarissa's career.

Their limousine arrived a moment later. It was an early two thousands Ford sedan with a nasty ding in the fender and a dark blue matte paint job instead of the traditional black.

Although Kimberly, short and petite, was clearly the frailest among them, Toby did not offer to help her heft the luggage into the trunk. Either he didn't want to steal the thunder of a job well done or he simply didn't care and was finding whatever he was reading on his phone to be of supreme interest.

"I was told by Mr. Teeks to keep discussion to a minimum, but I've got to say that I am such a fan," Kimberly said, resting the second suitcase above the spare tire and trying to wrestle it into position so the trunk could close.

Clarissa wasn't sure if there would be makeup or hair appliances provided, so she'd packed a few essentials, along with her own dryer and straightener.

"You can call me Clarissa. And I appreciate that, Kim," Clarissa said. To this Kim's face reacted with a mix of pride and revulsion, as if to say that she'd *never* stop calling her Ms. Lee. "About how far a drive is it, uh, to campus?"

Kimberly slammed the trunk shut and Clarissa tried not to wince at the resulting crunch. *They're just things. Conair builds their hair irons like brick shithouses, don't yell at the girl. She seems fragile.* Kimberly could very well be with her all weekend, and keeping the girl happy had a real bearing on Clarissa's comfort level.

"If traffic is okay, we should be there in two hours, tops," Kimberly said, her tone giving the impression that Clarissa knew *where* they were going, knew anything at all about this trip and con besides the fact that there was ten thousand dollars in it for her. Well, five thousand dollars. That advance check had already been spent.

Kim walked around the side of the car and opened the back door, then walked back to the curb to open the other side. The procedure was overly formal and a rental car shuttle beeped at her as she entered the street. Kim gave a small curtsy as she opened the second door, beckoning Clarissa to take a seat.

Toby looked up from his phone, seemed to regard the open doors as a kind of puzzle, then walked around to the far side of the car instead of sliding in with Clarissa.

"Are we all in?" Kimberly asked. Clarissa nodded and the girl closed the door for her.

From the parking lot, Clarissa could see what she assumed was the Cincinnati skyline in the distance. Kimberly pulled the car around the airport's terminals and parking structures and, instead of following the signs for the city, she took the highway south and drove deeper into Kentucky.

Well, that partially answered that.

Chapter Eight

Keith "Lumbra" Goldman—with a bag over his head, in the process of being transferred to who knew where—lay in the back of Rory's van and tried to think about his options.

Thinking was hard. Keith couldn't see but he guessed that Rory was driving. The stereo was tuned to Rory's particular mix of horrorcore rap. Which, if one weren't initiated, sounds a whole lot like a drum machine laid over someone speed-reading Jeffery Dahmer's grocery list. Keith would have called the music torture, if he weren't so recently familiar with *actual* torture.

Trying to fixate on something else helped to take his mind off the pain in his nose, which had begun to heal only to be knocked open by Rory during his latest beating. The wound burned and Keith was beginning to worry that it would never close and he would be whistling every time he exhaled for the rest of his life.

Not that "the rest of his life" seemed like it would be all that long an expanse of time.

So, in the back of the van, he thought about his options.

The three options were: beat them, join them, or run.

"Beat them" would include finding a way free of his restraints, acquiring or improvising a weapon, getting the drop on both Teeks and Rory and then finally subduing his captors (both the brains *and* the brawn). As much as Keith would like to flatter himself and say that he considered that an actual possibility, fighting back had been off the table from the start. Not only was Keith injured, dehydrated, and in a deep, life-scarring shock, but before any of this he had been a coward and a weakling, even at peak health.

Even if he weren't a weakling, he couldn't breathe without searing pain, his range of motion was extremely limited, and Rory was a monster. No. "Beat them" was out.

Run. Run seemed like the best option, but the opportunity hadn't presented itself yet, and there was still that nagging question of "Run to where?"

There were Ohio license plates on both Teeks' car and Rory's van, so he was probably in Ohio. There was nothing but woods outside of the house and garage, so there was no way of knowing for sure. Keith remembered every horror movie he'd ever seen. Not that they were meant to be how-to manuals, but not many of them had ended with the victim successfully running away through the woods.

With a similar level of shame that he'd nixed on fighting his kidnappers, Keith gave up on running.

He let his mind linger on the "join them" route. For all Rory and Teeks knew, Keith had already made the choice to join by collaborating with them to create Rory's costume, along with a few other mechanical gags they needed fabricated.

The normal-looking one, Teeks, seemed to have a fairly extensive base of knowledge about this stuff, even had Photoshop and CAD design skills. But Teeks was a busy man, constantly on his computer or talking to his girl on the phone. Keith guessed what Michael Teeks' needed from a "professional" like himself was less about lacking expertise and more about needing an extra pair of hands to help with the work. Not that Keith'd been given much of a choice, but he had put up no resistance. He'd been living and working alongside his captors for months now. It was possible that he'd already gone native without realizing it. Was that Stockholm syndrome or was that something else? Even at his most cogent it was hard for Keith to think.

There was no way of telling how long he'd been undergoing his brainwashing. Obviously, Keith didn't have a computer or phone out in the freestanding garage where he slept and tinkered. Additionally, the garage's 1995 Bud Light promotional calendar only helped him keep track of the days and didn't account for the hazy period of time he spent concussed when he first arrived.

The seasons were changing, though, so it was probably October, late-September at the earliest.

When they opened the van doors he could plead with them. Working fast would be crucial to ensure he wasn't immediately executed when they got him to where they were going—he assumed—to dump his body. In the darkness he tried to think of examples of how much help he could still provide to their enterprise. He made the costume and told them how to handle the blood. What did he have left to offer?

Back at the house, Keith had noticed that Teeks took two kinds of phone calls. The first was informal chats with employees (co-conspirators) like Rory and a woman he'd never seen named Kim. These were usually short, a time and place to meet, and then he took business calls that were a little harder to parse. On those calls the name MTY Productions kept coming up and there were discussions about numbers that Keith assumed were money. If it were one of the rare days where Keith was brought into the house to work, Teeks usually took the cordless phone out onto the porch where it was harder to hear. Keith took this to mean there was still a chance of him being let go alive. He hadn't seen these men kill anyone, only kidnap and intimidate. But both men smelled like cigarettes and neither smoked inside, so Teeks might not have been keeping anything from Keith on purpose. Those calls could have just been smoke breaks.

After months of listening to one side of Teeks' phone

conversations and the simplified talks that he'd have with Rory, Keith still wasn't quite sure *what* the two were planning, what Blood Camp Con was. But he had a rough idea, one he used his own life and career to put into context.

It was Keith Lumbra's father who'd gotten him into film.

Well, saying it like that didn't sound right. Everyone *liked* movies, they didn't need anyone to "get them into" them. Society at large did that work. But people who *really* enjoyed movies understood what Keith's interest level was like.

"He can miss a few days of elementary school. Boy's smart and can catch up on what's five times five tomorrow." His dad would provide that and similar excuses for Keith to play hooky and go to the movies.

Keith's dad preferred more serious fare, what Keith would later regard as Oscar bait, but he was fine encouraging his young son's interest in adventure films and sci-fi that bordered on insufferable kiddie stuff (he was a kid, after all). It was Keith's eventual turn toward horror that baffled his dad. In high school, during the car ride driving back from seeing Rob Zombie's debut *House of 1000 Corpses* (a movie he had since stopped defending at conventions), Keith's father had interrupted his son's praise of the film:

"I just don't know. Like, you're a good kid and I know that you like the things you do for the right reasons—as a film—but you've got to understand that I watch some of this shit and I wonder: what about the people watching for the wrong reasons? The ones *getting off* on it."

At the time the words had wounded Keith, a far deeper wound than his dad simply disagreeing about movie he liked, but he didn't understand why.

For most of his life, through all the films he'd made, cons he'd attended, the fake blood he'd waded through, and the flamewars he'd started online, Keith had held firm that his dad was wrong about horror, that he just didn't understand the genre or its fans.

Now, after spending weeks in the presence of Rory and Teeks, hearing the vague outline of what they had planned for their convention, Keith was horrified that part of his reaction to the plans was glee. On some level, their plans were *awesome*.

Rory and Teeks were the kind of horror fans Keith's father had worried existed and it turned out that maybe Keith *was* one of them.

On the cusp of connecting that piece of self-discovery to another, Keith was interrupted by a change in movement. Under him, the frame of the van rattled and during lulls in the stereo Keith could hear pebbles and dirt being flung up and bouncing off of the wheel wells.

The van had pulled off-road.

This cemented it: what had been a theory would now need to be put into practice.

He had to convince Teeks and Rory of his usefulness or they were going to kill him.

Well, actually, there was a fourth option that he hadn't considered before now: Keith could just give up and die.

Something about that appealed to him, especially since his broken nose had started to feel warm in recent days, the sensation almost a burn, an itch. Keith had heard once that if you made a triangle with your thumbs and pointer fingers and placed your nose in the center of that triangle you'd outline what dermatologists called your danger zone. You weren't supposed to pop any pimples that grew inside the danger zone, because if they went septic then those blood vessels could get infected and that infection could easily jump to your brain.

Maybe that was what was happening. Maybe his wounds had been torn open so many times that they'd gone putrid: sepsis of the danger zone would likely lead to insanity before resulting in death, no?

Did he have a fever?

The thought was interrupted by the van settling to a stop, the music cutting short.

Keith didn't want to die but he didn't feel up to arguing about it, so what he did was begin to cry.

The door opened and as the light spilled into the van Keith could see the crosshatching of the burlap in front of his eyes.

"Get up, we're here." Rory said.

"Please please please," Keith heard himself say, the words punctuated by sobs and becoming a kind of song.

"What's your fucking problem? Get. Up."

There was a slam—Rory kicking the bumper, maybe?—and Keith crawled onto his knees. The vibrations from lying on the floor had turned his left side into jelly, his muscles tingled and felt weak. Or maybe that was the shock and despair.

On his knees, trying to feel for the end of the van with his tied hands, Keith could sense Rory's impatience building. He was going to get hit for this, he knew it, but there was just no way to make himself move any faster.

"Oh for fuck's sake," Teeks said, his voice and footprints rounding the side of the van. Keith looked out and could *just* see their silhouettes behind the mesh of the bag.

Rory helped Keith with his indecision. The big man reached out and grabbed him by the shirt collar, pulling him out the door. The hard-packed dirt rose up to meet him.

Hitting the earth replaced the numbness in his limbs with pain. If he survived the next five minutes, he would take a second to be thankful that he was able to feel anything.

"Don't kill me," Keith said, finding his voice. "Help!" he began to shout, only once the word was out realizing how that could be misinterpreted as calling for help. "*I* can help!" he clarified his screams: "I can help you. Please don't kill me. Please don't."

There was the sound of laughter. It was Teeks'. Rory, for all of his childlike enthusiasm and lack of intelligence, was often the more serious of the two, at least around their captive. If the big man did laugh, he tried not to do it in front of Keith, like he was trying to prove what a tough guy he was, that he was the kind of kidnapper who wouldn't think twice about killing Keith.

There was a moment where no one spoke, a moment filled with the sound of Keith's nose whistle and that sound alone.

"Oh we know that you'll help," Teeks said.

Someone tugged off the bag and Keith wasn't able to get his eyes closed soon enough. The green-white of the sunlight blinded him and caused his headache to intensify.

"We're not going to kill you, Lumbra," Teeks continued. "If we did that then who else is going to hook up the cameras?"

Keith opened his eyes and watched as the out of focus world around him resolved itself into a campground: the cabins, the mess hall, the trees and the rope swings.

Oh God.

They were really doing it.

Chapter Nine

Teeks had been transparent with Marcus Lang and the actor had appreciated the candor.

Marcus wasn't the star of Blood Camp Con. He was a guest, but not the guest of honor. Oh no, he was meant as "cannon fodder."

Actors are cattle and should be treated as such, Marcus thought. Was that really a Hitchcock quote or was that apocryphal? Part of the mythologizing and lionizing of a fine director who was an even finer showman?

It didn't matter, because right now Marcus felt like cattle.

Blood Camp Con featured five guest stars, in addition to Ms. Clarissa Lee. Five supporting acts who were now all squeezed into a white van.

It was a van that would have had plenty of room if one of the seats hadn't been completely stripped of its upholstery, leaving just a rusty frame and springs behind.

Classy, class-A accommodations all the way at this convention.

Wedged between Gina Bright and Ivan Butinelli, Marcus was beginning to think he should have taken the messed up seat. Compared to being the meat in this white bread sandwich, Marcus would have preferred a few springs corkscrewing up his ass.

Marcus was the tallest of the three, so that he was riding the middle seat of the van's back row was a testament to how polite he was. He'd let Gina board the van first, with Butinelli holding out a hand and saying "after you."

Butinelli was either being a gentleman or didn't want to sit next to Bright.

He'd met both of them before, briefly, but for both of them briefly had been enough.

He did know about them, because it was part of his business to know about them and partly unavoidable, with all the cons he did.

Gina Bright had started out her career as a child star in a string of made-for-TV horror movies in the late seventies and early eighties, but would only refer to them as "psychological thrillers" after her breakout role. She was famous, but at conventions most casual fans knew to keep their distance. They all knew that she charged to take photos. Even if she wasn't behind her table when you took one, she'd coax you in with an open arm only to shake you down after. Like Marcus, most of the fans were able to smell the phoniness on her. Or maybe it was plastic-bottle gin.

Butinelli on the other hand—or elbowing into Marcus's ribs, as it was—started in porn, tried out legitimate acting in a couple of straight-to-video movies, then went back to porn once it became chic. He had his own brand of vodka and Marcus imagined that the liquor tasted like Drakkar Noir and forged STD checkup papers.

Butinelli regarded Gina Bright with an over-politeness that told Marcus he either really liked her or really didn't. Either way there was a shared history there that Marcus didn't want to be in the middle of. Even though he *literally* was in the middle of it at this moment.

Riding in the van's only functional second row seat was the eldest member of the group, Margery Clampton.

Margery had been a contemporary of Julie Adams. But where Adams was going swimming with the Creature from the Black Lagoon, a couple years later Margery was running for the hills pursued by irradiated centipedes. In bit roles Margery Clampton had shared the screen with John Agar and a young Vincent Price, but only the most diehard of nostalgic movie geeks would be able to name any of her starring roles.

Time had forgotten Margery Clampton, and Marcus would have pitied her if she seemed to have a shred of self-awareness and didn't strike him as (barely) latently racist.

Riding shotgun was someone young who Marcus didn't know. When they'd shaken hands in the airport parking lot she'd rattled a feature and TV credits to Marcus, but he hadn't been familiar with any of her stuff.

She was... damn. What was it? Tammy, but Tammy had been short for something... Tamera? That was enough, he didn't need to know her full name. They weren't here to make friends.

Instead of meeting a new member of the mysterious MTY's staff, it had been Michael Teeks himself who'd picked the group up from the airport. He was twenty minutes late, which was mildly concerning, and the van itself, too beat up to be a rental, was also a moderately strong red flag. But what was Teeks' grand plan? Kidnap a van full of C-listers? One of them an octogenarian who spent their whole drive so far complaining about the heat when it was 68 degrees and overcast?

Teeks' brief welcome speech detailed how there would be two different cabins for the men and the women. After that, the van went quiet.

Marcus closed his eyes. He wasn't tired and wouldn't be able to sleep, but it would help dissuade anyone from talking to him.

That attempt to fake-sleep his way through the trip lasted about five minutes, when he heard someone up ahead of him clear their throat and turn in their seat.

Tammy spoke.

"So your agents hooked this up?"

It wasn't clear who she was asking, but Marcus recognized the eagerness in her voice. She wasn't making small talk: she was taking the temperature of the talent in the room, possibly to see if she could make a connection and end up leapfrogging from one agent to another. If she had representation at all.

There was a fine line between leaning into oncoming success and desperation, and if Marcus were to guess he would say that Tamera Whatshername seemed perfectly content with crossing it.

Marcus opened his eyes to a squint, so he could continue to hide behind his eyelashes.

Margery either didn't hear Tammy or was deliberately ignoring her. The old woman continued to stare out the window.

It was Butinelli who spoke up first. Not, Marcus suspected, because he had any sage advice but because Tammy was cute.

"No, baby. I am my own people. In my opinion: that's the only way to be. At a certain point."

It was much to Marcus's shame that he recognized Butinelli's distinctive accent. It wasn't quite Italian and had a spoonful of 80s action movie Russian in it.

The "at a certain point" comment probably sounded better in the porn star's head than it did aloud, at least to Marcus. Butinelli wanted it to sound like: "once you reach a certain level" but to Marcus's ears it was "once you sink low enough, you can manage your own career death-spiral."

God. He hated that he was here, hated this business.

"I can't help you either." Gina said, seemingly prompted to enter the discussion by Butinelli's advice. "I got rid of my team, too, everyone except my publicist." She'd been playing with something inside her overlarge handbag for most of the trip, and from the smell of it, it was a flask.

"Oh, okay," Tammy said, turning back in the passenger's side seat. "I don't have anyone at the moment."

Marcus was just about to speak up, let it be known that he had
been approached by Teeks in person, but then Teeks did it for him.

"I hope this isn't talking out of school for anyone else," Teeks
began, seeming to slip into an accent he hadn't possessed when he'd
talked to Marcus back in New Jersey.

"Since MTY is a small company and we're, understandably, trying
to avoid getting SAG involved in our hirings: you were all targeted for
your lack of representation. I mean, you were targeted because of your
talents first and foremost. But not dealing with the guilds is good for us
in that it keeps costs down, and good for all of you because…well…*I'm*
not going to tell Uncle Sam what you're getting paid if you don't."

There was some polite laughter in the van, the loudest of it from
poor, naïve Tammy, but Marcus didn't participate. Instead he found
himself having to force his jaw to unclench before speaking up.

"Wait," he started, popping his elbows free from where they had
become wedged behind Gina Bright and Ivan Butinelli to lean forward.
"Why would you need to bother with *Screen* Actor Guild wages if there's
no screen? Are you planning on filming us?"

Maybe they had been shanghaied, but instead of a ransom they
were all being brought to appear in some shitty movie under the false
pretense that they were meeting up with fans.

Teeks made a noise that wasn't quite words, readjusted his grip on
the steering wheel, and then spoke up.

"I didn't mean to get you excited, Marcus. We *will* be filming most
of the events, but the footage will not be distributed for any commercial
reasons. Certain ticket packages included a souvenir DVD to be
compiled once we've had a chance to go through all the footage. We're
talking about a very limited pressing, less than twenty copies. It's all a
part of what you'll be compensated at the end of the weekend. And
your advance."

Marcus let the explanation hang there for a second and then

debated with himself whether he wanted to go to the mat over twenty DVDs.

"Oh, that's fine, I guess," Marcus said.

He looked over to Butinelli, who was scowling at him. The man who possessed a mushroomhead silhouette more famous than his jawline was giving Marcus a tsk-tsk for being so *vulgar* as to ask about their livelihoods.

Marcus glanced to Gina, but there was no backup coming from that direction. She didn't seem to be listening and just gave him a polite half-smile, the kind you give someone on the street when you're not really looking to stop and talk.

"I'm sorry I didn't mention being filmed earlier. There is a provision about it in your contracts." Teeks said. From Marcus's vantage he could barely see the man, just half his face, the white of his shirt sleeve as he guided the wheel around into a turn-off.

They were turning from the interstate to a smaller three-lane highway. Out the van's windows, signs of civilization were sparse, but there were still a few other cars on the road, and the occasional water tower or electrical pole broke up the horizon.

Tammy was the last to break the silence for the rest of the ride.

"This is so exciting, isn't it?" She didn't turn in her seat, just spoke it into the windshield and let the words wash over them, like she knew no one but Teeks had a chance of seconding her emotion.

Chapter Ten

Clarissa Lee ran her hands around the edge of the bathroom mirror. She tried to pull it towards herself, either to adjust it or open a hidden medicine cabinet, but brought her fingers back holding nothing but dust.

It figured.

The small mirror had been bolted to the wall and the lighting in this room was terrible.

It was probably for the best, anyway. Her apartment back in L.A. wasn't large, but still Clarissa owned two full-length mirrors. One in her bedroom and another propped beside her desk in the living room, and that was without counting the small vanity in the bathroom.

When she was in a certain kind of mood, she barely got any work done. Instead she would stare at herself, pick her skin, and pinch at the corners of her mouth and belly.

Clarissa was a natural blonde and outside of the occasional grey hair, she'd kept her pigment for fifty-four years, but it seemed these days the luster was fading. Aging was a slow-motion train wreck, one that it took a couple of cheap over-the-door mirrors from Ikea for her to truly appreciate.

The cabin's bathroom was cramped, but its fixtures had been recently replaced. Clarissa could smell the tang of fresh paint and grout.

Kimberly had told them that Blood Camp Con would be holding its inaugural year in a functioning summer camp. Well, functioning when it wasn't the off-season. Schools started in September, at least Clarissa thought they did, so there hadn't been anyone using these grounds for a couple of months, at least.

Looking around, Clarissa guessed that her cabin had either belonged to some administrator, the head councilor or scout master or whatever, or was utilized off-season as a posh rental by whoever ran the camp.

The cabin featured a plush reclining chair, a large work desk, and even a stone fireplace. There was a pile of black and white soot in the hearth that indicated the fireplace was more than decorative. To complete the woodsy aesthetic there was even a hunting rifle hanging over the mantle. If she were looking for clichés, she would have remembered what Chekov said about guns and fireplaces, but she was busy. As it was the gun made her feel uneasy, not because she was afraid it would go off but because something about it seemed familiar.

Why the cabin existed and how it was furnished didn't matter and Clarissa turned her attention back to her face and then let her eyes move down her neckline. She'd spent all day without a proper mirror and now she was going to take her time looking for problem areas.

The mirror was immobile, but if she stepped back and tilted her head to the light she could...

Clarissa dropped one strap of her night gown, revealing smooth white skin. Tenderly, she ran a hand up her side, the nail of her pointer finger measuring the crease between her armpit and breast.

55 years old, she began to think.

And then her quiet time was destroyed.

"You still need this light on?" Toby shouted from the other side of the bathroom door.

Clarissa was startled, then annoyed. "Yes! Don't touch it," she said.

She wanted to groan or scream in frustration, but instead sucked in her cheeks until her teeth began to throb and her face in the mirror went red.

It turned out that, since the fact that he'd been accompanying her hadn't been mentioned in her emails, Toby had been an unexpected plus-one for the con organizers. Organizers who had nowhere to put him.

Kimberly had offered him one of the bunks that the con's "campers" would be staying in, but had then revealed that he would need to share his space once the attendees started to arrive tomorrow morning.

Toby had said that would be fine, but Clarissa could read the concern on his face, could almost see inside of his nervous mind: the fact that he'd be alone tonight in a building meant to house a dozen or more teenagers and then packed in with fans tomorrow. Fans and their odors.

Or maybe that was her projecting onto Toby, her own feelings boomeranging back to her. Maybe *she* was the one who didn't want to be alone in the woods of Kentucky, no matter how nice the cabin or new the grout in the bathroom.

Whatever the explanation, Clarissa's desire to have a room of her own buckled and she said it would be fine for them to split the guest cabin, provided Toby was fine with sleeping in the armchair.

But now he had the audacity to try and dictate when she was going to bed? Looking to turn out the lights in the bedroom before she was ready?

She pulled the strap of her nightgown back over her shoulder. It wasn't the same to be inspecting her crow's feet and measuring moles in this tiny, unfamiliar mirror. Clarissa splashed some water in her face and began the process of removing her makeup. The water pressure was good. In fact it was too strong, when she turned both knobs there was no middle ground between "off" and "a loud, raging torrent of lukewarm water."

Ten minutes later, when she came back out of the bathroom, Toby was gone but she wasn't worried.

He did that sometimes, ghosting when he needed to take a call.

Clarissa laid her head down and listened to the crickets.

Hopefully he wouldn't wake her up when he came back in.

◆

It was funny. As Kimberly Yost looked into the one-way mirror, she didn't see Clarissa Lee as she was, the eighth of an inch of foundation stopping abruptly at her neckline, the skin of her breasts impossibly pale and too thin.

Instead Kimberly saw her as she appeared for most of the eighties: beautiful, young, and covered in blood.

When Clarissa Lee jumped, startled by her annoying little manager yelling from the other room, Kimberly jumped too. Her elbow knocked against the camera beside her and the feet of the tripod skittered across the concrete before she reached out to steady the equipment.

The room in which Kimberly stood had been recent construction. By halving the bathroom and taking a divot out of the living room they had installed an observation area. Standing here behind the mirror, someone was able to keep an eye on their guest of honor at all times.

Yeah, the camera alone would have worked just as well, but where was the fun in that?

Kimberly was glad she was getting to take the first shift, from what Daddy Teeks had told her about Rory: the place would probably be covered in gooey Kleenex by this time on Saturday. Wet tissues or worse...

Behind the glass, Ms. Lee had begun to run the tap. She bent to splash her face and her nightgown dipped. Kimberly *could* have stepped in front of the camera to block its view. She *could* have afforded the older woman some modesty, but this was good stuff, premium footage.

Kimberly felt her skin go flush. She thought about how in all her more recent films, Clarissa Lee had remained covered up. Had the lack of nudity been her decision? Had she gone Mormon or Scientologist? Or was it her manager's decision, to try to appear more like The Mom? Or did the directors and producers not want to see what a real woman looked like, stripped?

At the thought of him, Kimberly turned her mind to what to do about the manager. She took out her phone to text Daddy Teeks. Sliding through the lock screen, her phone made the distinctive Apple *clack!* She winced and flipped the switch that turned the phone to silent. Luckily the faucet was going on the other side of the glass.

She typed.

Do we need the manager? Lee doesn't seem to like him.

Hitting send, she looked back at the glass.

She'd never seen Clarissa Lee like this before. None of her fans had. This was private time.

With the corner of a damp washcloth, Ms. Lee pulled at the area under one eye. The white cloth came back cream-colored, with a slash of black at the tip from where it'd rubbed at her eyeliner.

Kimberly's phone buzzed. Even silent it was loud in the small, secret room. She would need to put it to complete "do not disturb" mode and make sure that Rory remembered to do the same when he came in here later.

Daddy Teeks: **No, don't need. Tell Rory. Boy needs to get it out of his system.**

Kimberly smiled. She took one last look at Ms. Lee through the glass. The star's face was an inelegant monster scowl as she scrubbed her forehead.

Careful not to linger, Kimberly squeezed out from the hidden door behind the tripod.

Once outside, she dialed Rory's number.

"Mr. Teeks said you get to start early. This is a dry run, though. No costume. None of the gags we've discussed. Meet us under camera twelve."

♦

Keith Lumbra watched the monitors switch as Rory yelled out numbers behind him.

"Two!"

Keith hit a button and the middle monitor, the largest of the five, stacked on top of the other four, switched to a night-vision view of the lake. There was a tower of canoes in the bottom left corner of the frame, each covered with a tarp and a speckling of fallen leaves.

"Fourteen!"

Keith held down the shift key and typed in the one and four keys. The monitor switched to their ultimate establishing shot: the camera rigged to the top of the sign spanning the driveway. The sign welcomed campers to Camp Rockwogh. Yesterday, Rory and Teeks needed to throw the vinyl "Blood Camp Con" signage up there, so while they had the ladder up, they'd sent Keith up to install one of the leftover security cameras atop the sign.

Using his trackball mouse, Keith was able to control the zoom. He rolled the ball down as far as it could go to widen up the shot. The equipment was clumsy and outdated. Keith hadn't used a trackball since high school when he'd taken Television Production. Back then he hadn't been your typical A/V club nerd: but he had needed access to the equipment if he was going to start dipping his toes in filmmaking.

Camera fourteen's vantage was a good twenty-five feet above the road in and out of camp. From there they could see almost the entirety of the camp. There was the main stage, the three cabins flanking it, the roof of a fourth cabin separate from the rest, and the corner of the administrative building/cafeteria where Keith and Rory were currently sitting.

Well, Keith was sitting, one of his ankles strapped to his rolling office chair by a bike chain. Rory was standing behind him, sticking his fingers onto the monitors and leaving greasy smudges.

Keith wanted to tell him to stop touching the equipment, but that was the kind of insubordination that could get him clapped over the ear so hard that he began to bleed.

It had happened before.

"Now go to," Rory began and put a hand on Keith's shoulder. The hand was so heavy. And it didn't feel like the big man was leaning into him, that ache in Keith's muscles was just from the weight of the man's enormous arm with no additional pressure. The message Keith took from this: Rory didn't even have to be trying in order to hurt Keith.

"Tubular Bells" began to play. The song was Rory's ringtone, and the big man stopped giving directions. Before coming to live with Teeks and Rory, it'd been a long time since Keith had heard a custom ringtone and the experience did nothing to shake the feeling that Rory was an enormous, impressively-stubbled teenager.

Once the phone was out of his pocket, Rory pushed down and away from Keith, the suspension of the roll chair letting out a hiss as it was compounded. Keith glided to a stop with his stomach hitting up against the table. The monitors rattled against the hit and Rory shushed Keith.

"Hello," Rory said into the phone. Keith didn't turn in his chair and tried his best not to look like he was eavesdropping. Keith had come to the decision that he would brook no further resistance to his captors plans. And if he wasn't planning on resisting, why would he need to eavesdrop?

It was no use, though, because this close, in the quiet of the control room, he could hear the female voice on the other end of the line. It was difficult to pick out every word, but he knew it was Kimberly on the other side of the conversation, and he definitely heard "meet me" and "Teeks."

"Sure thing, be there soon. But no mask?"

Rory paused and listened to the response. Not that Keith himself was exactly a quiet breather these days, with his split nose, but he noticed that Rory's own breath was heavier now. It was the same pattern of respiration Keith's dog used to assume in the pauses between waiting for the ball to be thrown and the fetching.

Rory was beside himself with excitement. The big man could hardly hold it in. Keith could tell.

"So *a* mask but not *the* mask? Cool. I like it. See you soon," Rory said, then rushed to add: "But wait. Wait…should the geek switch on the phone thing?"

The phone thing, Keith thought and instantly caught a touch of nausea. The jammer had worked with the two test phones, but those had both been using the same provider and who knew how long and how far the coverage would span once they switched it on for good. Keith was a far cry from an electrical engineer, but he'd been able to assemble what Teeks had asked for after watching some YouTube tutorials. If the device didn't work then it would end up being Keith's fault.

Rory waited for a response. Keith did too, keeping his eyes on the keyboard in front of him.

"Makes sense, it shuts us down too. Okay, see you soon," Rory said and hung up.

In the reflection of one of the smaller monitors, each one a slightly out-of-date glass CRT TV, Keith could see Rory jump and punch the air. It was the fist-pump of a pro athlete. Rory's boots slammed back down, causing the floor boards to creak and shake.

"It's happening! It's happening," Rory said, spinning Keith around in his chair so he could enjoy the action. This was the happiest Keith had ever seen his captor. "I just need a..." Rory started but then trailed off. Rory paced the small room, which must have served as a kind of counselor's break room, judging from the mini-fridge and worn couch pressed against one end.

The folding table, hard drives, keyboard, mouse, walkie talkies, and monitors had been a recent addition to the break room, as the camp had lacked any kind of closed circuit equipment.

Rory crossed to the couch and took up one of the smaller cushions laid across the arm rest.

He tore at the corner of the pillowcase, straining against the material until he realized that there was a zipper. He undid the zipper, removed the pillow from the thicker, floral pillowcase, and threw the case over his head. Now hooded, Rory dug both hands into his pockets and rooted around for a second before coming out with a pocket knife.

Clumsily peeling out the blade without lifting the pillowcase from over his eyes, Rory put one hand up to his face and began to carve himself an eyehole.

Please stab yourself in the face, Keith found himself wishing, only to put a hand to his lips to ensure that he wasn't saying the words aloud. It had been a long two days on top of an even longer few months. There was no way of telling how fried his brain is, how loopy he'd gone. Even as recent as last night, Keith had found himself waking up screaming for his mother, a nightmare that had crossed into reality and had earned him a late-night beating from Rory.

"How do I look?" Rory asked, turning to Keith.

Keith didn't say anything just croaked out an extended "Uhhhhhhh."

"Spit it out, I've got to go," Rory said, reaching over Keith's shoulder and pulling down a loop of excess coaxial cabling from the top of one monitor.

"You look great!" Keith said, his voice shaky. He hadn't been required to talk a lot recently, just "yes" and "no" mostly.

The truth was that Rory looked like Rory with a flowery pillowcase over his head, but who was Keith to judge that the look wasn't fearsome? He was scared as hell of Rory, no matter how many flowers he had on his head.

"Good, follow me on the screen, but have camera twelve ready to go. Make sure you're recording. And, Lumbra?"

"Yes?" Keith asked, weirdly feeling like Rory was going to tell him something positive. Like "keep up the good work" or something similar.

"Don't fuck up," Rory said, testing the strength of the cabling by tugging it taut. He lifted up the edge of his mask with one thumb, to show Keith he was smiling. Then, before Keith could pull away, Rory struck out with the cable like a whip, connecting with the back of Keith's left hand.

Rory was out the door before the welt had a chance to turn white and Keith already had his seat turned around, tracking his movement with the cameras.

The pain in his hand was nothing.

♦

Toby Givens was short, but he did not seem light.

At least, he didn't look that way to Kimberly. But she wasn't the one lifting the short man off his feet in front of Cabin Three.

Cabin Three was that one…Falcon? Eagle? She couldn't tell what the bird on the sign was supposed to be, couldn't remember what they'd called it. It was late and her time at Camp Rockwogh was a fuzzy memory. Kimberly had a young-looking face, and played that feature up with the way she dressed and acted, but in reality she was closing in on thirty. It had been many summers since camp.

She had never returned as a counselor, herself, but that was probably how the older kids had thought about the cabins: One, Two, and Three. Not as Deer, Bear, and whatever bird of prey it was that was carved into the sign above them. She thought the counselors must think of the buildings in a similar way to how waitresses knew the floor plans of their restaurants by table numbers.

Toby had answered the door quickly, which was good because it was better to get him outside while Ms. Lee was still in the bathroom, cleaning her face.

Kimberly had anticipated more difficulty getting him to follow her out into the woods, late at night, but the manager had come along with minimal fuss.

"I hate to be doing this to you, especially this late, but Mr. Teeks needs to see you. I don't know what it is, but he said that there seems to be an issue with Ms. Lee's contract," she said, holding a finger in the belt loop on her shorts. The weather could have gone either way, planning this far into October, but it had stayed unseasonably warm. A good omen, surely, and one that meant she got to rock her shorts in the fall.

The manager wore a white undershirt and long, old-man boxers that partially covered his knees. He would not have looked out of character wearing ankle garters, but alas, he had none.

"What kind of contract problem?" he asked. "She's signed."

"Like I said, I don't know. All this stuff is new to me. He just called and told me that he wanted to talk to you. It sounded technical and well," she held her hands out, playing the "I'm just a P.A." card again and setting it down with conviction.

She was just a *wittle giwl from the stwicks*, what would she know about the industry?

Instead of going back inside to put pants on, he just walked out into the night, closing the door behind him. Maybe Toby Givens had the capacity to annoy, but he was willing to work for his client, any time of night.

"He's just a short walk away. Our team's working through the night to put the finishing touches on one of the attendee cabins." Kimberly held her hand out to guide him, a *right this way* motion.

Where Toby Givens produced the phone from, she didn't want to know (the sweatband of his boxers?), but the moment they hit the footpath leading to the center of camp, the older man had his Blackberry out and switched onto flashlight mode.

That could be a problem. Not a huge one, but a problem.

As they walked, Kimberly looked up. The night sky was full of stars. It was the reason everyone gave for liking the country, going out into the woods to avoid the light pollution, but that didn't make it any less true, or the light-show of a clear night any less awe-inspiring.

Kimberly glanced back and Toby was staring into his phone, scrolling through messages while the flashlight was still on. *Kill your battery much, guy?*

Hmmm. Kill. *Ki Ki Ki Ma Ma Ma.*

She smiled to herself and cleared her throat in order to make sure Toby knew to follow her down the right fork in the path, towards the darker part of the camp.

Kimberly had chosen to meet at Cabin Three because it was the furthest from the rest of the guests. The rest of them had only just arrived a couple of hours ago, then been shown to the guest cabin (Deer, er, One). It was likely that one or more of them weren't yet asleep, especially if any of them were keeping California time. She hadn't yet had the opportunity to meet any of them or to debrief with Daddy Teeks. There was so much to get done before tomorrow.

Well, Cabin Three was secluded *and* Kimberly had a pretty good memory of where that camera had been set up: it had two large trees framing the shot, and the cracked-white paint of the cabin would provide a silhouetting effect.

"Here we are. He should be inside," she said.

Toby looked up from his phone and then looked to Kimberly. He had an expression on his face that was polite but still incredulous.

Yes, she *was* acting suspicious. And no, the lights weren't on inside Cabin Three, the Eagle, they could both see that.

"Doesn't look like he is in there," Toby said, peering into the dark cabin. "Why don't you call him?"

It was a pity. Cabin One—the one with the carved Deer placard— would have been more appropriate. Toby was doe-eyed, confused but also confused about why he should be confused. And was that a little bit of fear she saw in his expression?

"Just do it already," Kimberly said, finally dropping her voice to her normal register, not the character of the "production assistant" that she'd been wearing for the last six or so hours. How these actors did this all day was beyond her. It was exhausting.

Toby scrunched up his face, as if to ask "just do what already?" but she hadn't been talking to him.

Rory tossed the loop of—what was that? Rope? Some kind of cabling?—around Toby's neck and the smaller man was lifted off the ground. His Blackberry slipped from his fingers and fell end over end, landing with the LED flashlight shooting up into the sky. The tiny but powerful light threw strong shadows onto the faces of the manager and his attacker.

Rory strained and lifted higher, groaning. The big man laughed through the exertion. His elbows dug into Toby Givens' spine and forced the manager's chest forward into a position that would have been uncomfortable for a man of any age.

Toby was incredibly quiet. There was no way for him to scream with all his weight being leveraged against his windpipe.

Kimberly wouldn't go so far to say that she was disappointed, but she would agree that the kill was remarkably uncinematic.

Toby just hung there, his arms and legs not only *not thrashing*, but barely moving at all. The weight and the sudden jerk of the garrote had been too much, maybe. The cable had worked a sharp divot into the man's throat, sealing up not only air but blood flow.

Kimberly took a step back to ensure that she wouldn't be in the hidden camera's shot. She tried to think of a single choking scene in all of cinema that had been this quiet.

Rory's pillowcase mask looked ridiculous, but maybe in the black and white of the surveillance footage the floral pattern wouldn't read quite as...flowery. That was fine, though. All of cinema's killers underwent some kind of transformation process. This version of Rory was larval. They would make him better.

◆

Keith Lumbra kept his hand on top of the tower of hard drives and watched the murder unfold on the monitor.

He could feel the spin of the drive through his palm, feel the warmth traveling up from the rest of the equipment as the machine kept up. The warmth helped take his mind off the pain on the back of his hand. The pain was all over his body, in fact, starting at his nose and echoing outward to his extremities.

The stack of hard drives was converting raw data into memory, taking in every detail from the three camera feeds Keith currently had set to record. The hard drive was taking down more information than anyone would ever need, but that was the point. Keith had been instructed not to miss anything, and he wasn't going to. Teeks wanted coverage and he would get it.

One camera rolled on an inferior set-up where only a sliver of Rory's back and shoulder could be seen, but it would still come in handy if either party moved.

Camera Fourteen, the establishing shot, was still being recorded in case Rory carried the body away with him when he was done, crossing through the center of camp. He wouldn't, Keith guessed. It would be better to dump the poor bastard in the woods.

And then there was the main event.

Camera Twelve was pointed to catch the rear of Condor Cabin, with a few extra degrees of forest to either side. Each camera had zoom functionality, but rather than risk Rory or his prey dipping out of the frame, Keith was keeping a fairly wide angle. He kept Kimberly, who didn't have a mask to hide her identity, just off screen. He could crop the frame later, pan and scan it, if need be.

You're directing again, said a voice inside him.

Well, he shouldn't be that dramatic. The voice was Keith's own, maybe a little more of a whisper than his usual internal monologue. There was no demon hiss to it, no particular malevolence at all, simply a gentle touch of sarcasm.

Keith Lumbra rides again. The man simply can't stop making movies. Kidnap him and guess what? He'll find a way to make art! Would this be his final picture? Would it make any sense without rolling live sound? And would he be around to sit in the edit bay?

He thought about the money that Teeks must have spent to put this all together. It was a crazy amount to invest, especially for a man who didn't seem to spend any money on his car.

The travel expenses alone must have dwarfed the entire

production budget of *Incest Virgin Massacre*, Keith's latest feature before the abduction, though he'd been working on two more that hadn't yet been completed.

Was there anything he could do to stop this madness from where he was sitting?

No, nothing, not in as bad a shape as he was, physically.

He drummed his fingers on the hard drive and watched Rory lower the smaller man's lifeless body to the ground. The corpse's knees folded in under, leaving the body in the position of an awkward prayer.

No. All Keith could do now was direct. He had to document what was going on here. Bearing witness would be his contribution. Wasn't that how most extreme horror guys (and they were all guys) tried to justify the movies they made? *I'm not endorsing the* content. *It's fiction. But it tells you something about the world, man.*

Keith could lie and say that he was doing such a good job of logging coverage for the authorities, so that they could build some kind of hypothetical case. But it was more than that.

He was doing this for his audience, one last time.

Chapter Eleven

It was hard for Marcus to sleep. Yes, the 'talent' had their own cabin. But the level of amenities provided had been greatly exaggerated when Teeks had pitched him in the supermarket.

Instead of a separate, free-standing building for the male and female guests, a flimsy canvas partition had been constructed in the middle of the cabin, leaving four beds in their side, six for the women's.

No. Not beds, bunks. Bunk beds.

Teeks had showed the guests to the door, wished them a goodnight, and then begged his leave. They'd entered, and Marcus saw another opportunity for his politeness to screw him out of comfort. It was unlikely that he'd have another roommate besides Ivan Butinelli, but Marcus threw his shoulder bag onto the top of the nearest bunk and laid his jacket across the floor-level bed, marking his territory.

He wasn't taking any chances. He wasn't going to risk sleeping on a twin bed suspended six feet off the ground.

"Hey, you up?" a voice said in the dark cabin.

The whisper took Marcus by surprise. Not that Ivan Butinelli was snoring or anything, but he'd assumed that the porn star would have had an easier time falling asleep. It bothered Marcus that they were in a sparsely populated children's summer camp, but what little he'd gleaned about Butinelli's character made Marcus think the man was less than introspective.

"Yeah, I'm up," Marcus replied, not whispering himself. He was too self-conscious that hushed conversations after lights out was the exact kind of thing that 12-year-olds did at sleepovers.

"Oh," Ivan's voice said from the other side of the dark room. He sounded disappointed. "I was trying to see if the girl was up, actually. Tammy. I thought you were asleep, man."

"Oh. Makes sense," Marcus said, no real reason why he should feel so embarrassed.

There was a long pause while, presumably, Ivan waited for a reply from the other side of the partition. None came and Marcus heard the other man shift in his bed, place his feet on the floor and cross the room to the window over the door.

Marcus stretched his feet out, pushing his head up on his pillow by pressing against the bed frame. He was unnerved to see Butinelli outlined in moonlight. The man was wearing underwear brief*er* than boxer briefs. It was a body builder's Speedo, but Butinelli lacked the toned physique that was meant to accompany such a garment.

Butinelli wasn't completely out of shape, but struck Marcus as the kind of guy who hit the gym only for the chest press and some bicep curls. No legs, no cardio. He could almost hear the man's excuse in his head: *I get enough cardio at work. Har har!*

Butinelli leaned into the door, face to the window. His gut hung over his waistband and cast a shadow over his lower half. That was good: the shadow granted partial modesty to the man's claim to fame.

Marcus didn't really know much about how the porn industry worked, but there was no way the belly was helping Butinelli's career. It was certainly not what Marcus wanted to look at when he closed the shades and turned on privacy mode on his browser. The gut itself could be the reason why he was here right now, in the woods of Kentucky, instead of crunching on handfuls of Cialis in a Burbank McMansion.

"See anything?" Marcus asked.

"Trees and more trees," the other man replied.

"It doesn't creep you out, just a little, that there are so few of us here in the middle of nowhere? That we had to be driven so far once we landed?" Marcus paused. No answer came so he elaborated. "I mean, who in their right mind could be coming to this thing? No fan of mine, I don't think."

"Eh, not really scared. This," Butinelli started. He waved a hand at the window, the pale skin of his underarm becoming a slash of reflected moonlight from where Marcus lay. "This is Mickey Mouse forest. At least to me. I grew up north of Kiev. If you want to see scary fuckin' wilderness: drive an hour north or east of my hometown. This is nothing. There we have wolves. Your wolves here? In zoos and parks? They're like dogs. Our wolves? They have to be big so they can take down the wild pigs. Those are scary, too."

"Kiev? So that means you're full Russian...er," Marcus tried to consult what little geography he knew. "Ukrainian? Does that mean the Italian thing's a stage name?"

"I didn't say that," Butinelli said, causing further confusion to Marcus' questions about his lineage. When he was done talking he pinched at a patch of razor burn at the bottom of his stomach, working at either a blemish or ingrown hair with one of his fingernails. It was the kind of thing most people did when they were sure no one was watching. But Butinelli had made a career out of being filmed doing something most people considered private, so maybe his barometer was a little screwy.

It was strange and terrible how much Marcus's eyes had adjusted to the starlight, that he could watch this.

They sat quietly for a moment, Marcus sitting up with his back against the pillow headboard, finally feeling the weight of sleep pressing against him. Not that Butinelli had put him at ease, telling him about the forests of Ukraine, but at least now there was someone standing watch.

"Now *that's* creepy," Butinelli said, breaking the silence an indeterminate amount of time later. The words caused Marcus to nod his chin against his chest and realize that he'd been in the middle of falling asleep. His lower lip felt wet and he pressed a hand to his sternum to make sure he hadn't drooled onto himself. He had, but only a little.

"What is?" Marcus asked, finding it difficult to get the words out, he was so tired.

"There's a guy out there dragging a prop body through the woods," Butinelli said and pointed out the window. "He must be setting up for tomorrow."

"Weird," Marcus said, feeling so much more comfortable as he squared his shoulders with the pillow, the memory of the exchange mixing itself up with a dream as Ivan Butinelli said one last thing Marcus didn't catch before slipping away into unconsciousness.

In his dream it sounded like, "Someone's hauling a body."

Chapter Twelve

Clarissa rarely used nighttime mode on her phone. She only ever considered turning it on when Toby was in one of his excitable deal-making moods and it seemed likely that he would attempt to call her in the middle of the night. Nighttime mode silenced text messages that would otherwise vibrate and sent all incoming calls to voicemail.

But with Toby sleeping in the same room, she hadn't thought to turn the feature on.

After all, outside of the little old lady who ran her dry cleaner and Merry Maids, Toby was the only person who called her with any regularity. Maybe she should try internet dating.

Considering that no one called her, she was surprised to be woken at 8 a.m., not by the sunlight sneaking around the cabin's drapes, but by the buzz of two texts, one after the other.

In a paralytic half-sleep, she reached over to silence the phone, but wound up reading the text anyway.

Hey. Soooo sorry but there's been a family emergency. That's what that call was last night I need to

The message ended, then continued.

Get back to LA. I had Mr. Teeks arrange me a ride to the airport. Break a leg! Good weekend!

This early in the morning, it was hard for Clarissa to make much sense out of the messages, but she had no problem getting the gist on her first time through and no problem articulating a feeling to go along with that understanding:

Fuck, she thought.

Toby had family? She was 99% certain that he was an unmarried only-child, but she couldn't remember if one or both of his parents were still alive.

The thought that Toby, no spring chicken, had parents who certainly had to be elderly was more depressing and vivid than anything should have been this early in the morning. Clarissa imagined Toby taking care of his mother, an old woman of ninety-something who maybe even lived with Toby. The amount of time he spent on Clarissa meant that he was splitting his time between two old ladies, maybe even neglecting his poor, arthritic, possibly demented mother in favor of running to Jamba Juice for Clarissa. What if the family emergency had been his mother dying?

She knew that it was a self-centered leap to make, but with only Clarissa left for Toby to take care of, what kind of Norman Bates relationship would the two of them form in her twilight years?

Considering the circumstances, how she hadn't even known the most cursory facts about his life, she couldn't be mad at him. But neither did Clarissa relish the thought of making it through the weekend alone.

Not really awake but not really resting, she lay in bed for another hour. The hour ended when the squeal of a bullhorn roused her.

"Testing. Testing. Can you hear me in the booth? Thumbs up?"

It was Kimberly's voice, amplified for maximum annoyance.

For a "production assistant" at the camp, the girl seemed to be doing an awful lot of work. Maybe they didn't know what the term meant in Kentucky. Kimberly's main concern should have been learning how the guests took their coffee and when she needed to go feed parking meters. Full stop. And there were probably no meters out in the woods of Kentucky, anyway. So just the coffee then.

"Good morning, *campers!*" she giggled at this salutation, then corrected herself: "I'm only kidding. Good morning *honored guests!* Breakfast will be served in the main building in just fifteen minutes. The first group of attendees isn't expected to arrive until ten-thirty or eleven. Which means you'll have time to eat in peace and relax. Get to know each other. And a chance to get into character. I'll see you there!"

Clarissa sat up, considered showering, but then considered how nice breakfast sounded. She couldn't allow herself to get her hopes up, though. She'd eaten enough "complimentary" green room breakfasts in her life to know that what usually passed for a banquet at these things was a communal bowl of dry cereal and stack of day-old pastries.

Her hunger successfully tamped down by lowered expectations, Clarissa once again turned her mind to that all-important question: *Where the hell am I?*

She and Toby had been given a brief tour yesterday, which mostly consisted of Kimberly pointing at buildings and saying things that Clarissa only half-listened to. Kimberly was more concerned with camp history and anecdotes of her time at Rockwogh as a kid than she was at explaining the actual geography or amenities. This morning, it would be good to get an actual lay of the land and meet the rest of the 'professionals' she'd be spending the next two nights and three days with.

She couldn't help to wonder who else the organizers of Blood Camp Con had been able to rope into this shit.

♦

Kimberly was able to match Toby Givens'—surprisingly feminine—style of text messaging fairly well when typing her cover story into the dead man's Blackberry.

Most of the manager's texts started with some kind of apology, so Kimberly made sure that hers did too.

Composing the message was fun, kind of like a creative writing assignment, but the phone's small directional pad gave her trouble and she ended up splitting the text into two separate messages. A Blackberry? Who still used these things? Was his Palm Pilot in the shop?

Creating the paper trail was easy, but crawling around Ms. Lee's cabin while she was sleeping and gathering up all of her manager's belongings had proved slightly more difficult. It was a challenge, to be sure, but a thrilling one.

There was no way of telling if Clarissa Lee was a heavy sleeper. That was not something a fan could look up on an IMDB page. But Kimberly was pleased to find that Clarissa was sleeping soundly enough after a day of travel.

Sneaking up behind the arm of the chair and cinching Toby's pant pockets closed so his keys and change didn't jingle as she removed them was maybe the riskiest part. She folded the pants and laid them over top of Toby's computer bag, easier to locate in the dark since Kimberly had handled it earlier in the day.

When Kimberly was finished, her eyes adjusted to the darkness, she scanned the room, making sure there was nothing left. When she'd left him, Toby's corpse had been wearing his glasses, but she found the case for them on Ms. Lee's bedside table.

In order to retrieve the glasses case she had to get very close to the bed. She could hear the gentle whoosh of Ms. Lee's breath against the blanket. Ms. Lee had brought the sheets up around her face, cocooning her head. It was warm in the room, but it must have been even warmer *inside* those sheets with Clarissa Lee.

It was as close as she dared get, but Kimberly chanced an extra second in the room to hold the back of her hand over the chimney in the sheet. She kept the hand there, curling her fingers around the warm air caused by her favorite movie star's respiration.

In, out.

She cupped her hand and scooped it up to her nose, the way she'd seen some snobs drinking in the smell of wine in movies. Wafting. That was the word, she was wafting in Clarissa Lee's exhalation and finding the experience intoxicatingly sweet and sour, toothpaste that'd warn off and begun to succumb to the mouth's baseline bacteria.

It was a pleasure to be this close, to feel and smell this sweetness.

It was going to be a great weekend.

"Wow," someone said behind Kimberly, breaking her from her remembrance of last night. The voice nearly echoed against the high ceilings of the empty cafeteria.

Kimberly turned to see a young woman around her own age.

It took a certain kind of fuzzy vision to place her, the way familiar faces don't look familiar when they're in a different setting and with different makeup. The first guest to arrive in the cafeteria was Tamara Reyes, current Indie horror darling. She'd only done one film, and she wasn't the star, but afterwards she'd hit the con scene in a big way. Kimberly had never seen her in action, but supposedly she was very good to fans. Maybe that was because she was compensating for something.

"Is all of this for us?" Tamara asked, motioning to the hotplates arrayed along one side of the lunch room.

"All you can eat," Kimberly said, then tilted her head to watch more guests walk through the main building's double doors. Not that Tamara Reyes wasn't exciting, but Kimberly was not a fifteen year old boy. No, her hero worship was reserved for...

Marcus f'ing Lang!

Mr. Lang shouldered into the room looking groggy. The early morning stupor lasted only a moment, though, because his nostrils flared and his expression changed as he caught scent of the food.

Mr. Lang's immortal turn as Roger Powers, a southern police chief who stayed Barry White-cool in the midst of a demon invasion of his town, had been one of Kimberly's first screen crushes. These days there was a little salt mixed in with the pepper of Mr. Lang's thick mustache, but he kept his head shaved so that was about the extent of the changes he'd gone through. His was a timeless handsomeness.

Either that or he kept a better self-care regimen than the rest of the guests.

His eyes met Kimberly's and he smiled at her. *He actually smiled at her.* Her day was already made. It was hard to imagine that things could get any better, even though she knew they were going to.

"So, we, ahhh, can just go for it?" he asked in that trademark deep voice. It was just north of Isaac Hayes in register and Kimberly found herself suddenly wondering if Marcus Lang had ever done any singing, himself. Or was that racist to think? Or, if not racist, was it problematic? Mr. Lang had a plate already in his hand and was preparing to spoon himself out some scrambled eggs, but asked his question again when he got no answer, before digging in.

"Yes, sure," Kimberly nodded and blushed, waving the attention away from herself, like his stare would melt her if he held it too long.

Next to stumble in—literally—was Gina Bright. Ironically, Bright held the arm of Margery Clampton, someone twice her age who seemed to have no trouble navigating the door's threshold.

"Come in, come in, please take a plate and enjoy," Kimberly said, taking up a position by the door, getting clear of the most direct path to the food.

Everything was still warm and fresh, but it hadn't been made on sight. The kitchen would have needed a full staff to pump out this much food.

Daddy Teeks had driven the pancakes, bacon, and eggs in this morning and Rory had helped set up, his size making quick work of carrying the aluminum trays. Whatever was left after the guests had eaten would become the attendees' lunch. Although it looked good and there was plenty of it, Kimberly understood that this was for their guests. She was fine with the peanut butter and jelly she'd stashed in the control room's office.

"Thanks," Gina Bright said. Kimberly was hit with the astringent smell of alcohol rolling off of the woman, which explained the stumbling.

Ivan Butinelli and Ms. Lee were the last to arrive. Mr. Butinelli surged in front of her to the top of the steps in order to make a big show of holding the door.

"After you, Bella," Butinelli said, his accent all over the place, even inside of just three words. Kimberly giggled at this, also at the thought that it was Gina Bright whose name sounded like a porn star's. The actual porn star in attendance had a hard-to-pronounce name more suited to a plumber or deli worker than someone who frequently played plumbers and deli workers, however unconvincingly. *Extra meat on that foot-long, ma'am?*

Yes, she'd seen his most widely known "straight film" *Amphibian Hell* and enjoyed it just fine, for what it was, a sub-Full Moon puppet and tit fest. But she'd also perused a few of Butinelli's other works, the films he'd made outside of the horror genre.

Oh, she'd done it for research purposes. Of course.

It was surreal to now be seeing a man she'd seen so much of on screen, in the flesh.

From her vantage at the corner of the big room, Kimberly watched the guests walk down the buffet line and then take their seats. Unprompted, the guests congregated at one of the middle tables by the room's largest window. Kimberly kept her arms folded behind her waist trying to keep a professional, quasi-military attention. This wasn't because she thought of herself as some kind of shock trooper, but because otherwise she wouldn't have known what to do with her hands.

The lunch tables and attached benches were big enough that all six guests could sit comfortably at one. Kimberly turned her chin up and looked to the small bubble that housed the surveillance camera. Yes, this first breakfast, with all of the guests together was being preserved for posterity, but there was no record of it at ground-level. Not in the color or high resolution that she would be able to capture with her camera phone.

She reached for her phone, her heart pumping. She realized both the social and professional indiscretion she was about to commit.

"Everyone," she said. Her voice cracked and she spoke too low to be heard over the polite conversation that had begun to blossom among them. She cleared her throat and tried again: "Excuse, me, everyone!"

They all turned to her and she held out her phone. And why not preserve this? It was the last time they'd all be together, right?

"Just a quick photo, if you don't mind. Please lean in."

At the table, Tamara Reyes daintily covered her mouth to finish chewing, Gina Bright rolled her eyes, and the rest of the stars leaned in and smiled, offering no resistance. It was just one little picture, after all, and the guests seemed to be in good spirits. Oh the wonders of breakfast sausage.

"Kimberly!" a familiar voice sounded from behind her, causing her finger to falter on the shutter. She took the photo, but the shock of being caught had caused her to shift the focal point to the floor instead of the table. The picture turned out blurry and under exposed as a result of her fumbling hands.

What a perfect time for Daddy Teeks to walk in on her. She glanced back up to the surveillance camera. *Or had it been a coincidence?*

"Sorry about that everyone, we know you just want to eat in peace, but it's difficult for us to hold back our impulses," he said. "We are all fans, of course, Kimberly included. But we did make a promise to you that Blood Camp Con would be different."

"I'm sorry," Kimberly said, almost finishing by saying 'Daddy,' but knowing that that was their private word. Others wouldn't understand and it was best to keep their relationship strictly professional. At least while in public.

Simultaneously, the majority of the guests all said variations on "it's no trouble at all." Excepting Ms. Clampton, but that could be forgiven because the old woman now looked unaware that anything had transpired at all.

That was nice that they were so quick to forgive Kimberly. The guests were nice. They were almost her friends.

"I just wanted to stop in and give you an update. When you're finished with breakfast, there will be about two hours for you to get ready, shower, enjoy the campus, etcetera before we ask that you gather near the stage for the opening ceremonies," Daddy Teeks said, adjusting the waistband of his pants in a way that seemed to indicate he didn't really need to adjust, but was somehow getting into character with the gesture. "Most of the campers will have arrived by then and there will be a short presentation on what the weekend entails and the schedule of events."

The guests all watched Daddy Teeks as he spoke, but they did not entirely pause their breakfast, the occasional slice of bacon still consumed with hushed crunches.

"Before you go your separate ways, I do need to ask Ms. Reyes to stay behind," Daddy Teeks met the young woman's eyes. She was the room's *other* young woman and as he spoke to her a strong wave of jealousy hit Kimberly, unsettling her stomach. "In order to discuss the issue that I'd emailed you about last week?"

Tamera Reyes nodded and Butinelli faux-whispered to her. "Ooooo, staying after class," Butinelli said and the young starlet became red in the face, causing everyone else at the table to chuckle. There was a sour note in the sound, though, the immediately jovial nature of the breakfast beginning to ring false for Kimberly. Were they really all such good friends from seeing each other once a year (if that) at fan conventions or were all actors adept at assuming the look and feel of happiness, of companionship?

"Kimberly, let's let our guests eat," Daddy Teeks said, the command wiping away the doubt that was beginning to cloud her thoughts and turning her mind back to the fact that she'd just taken an unsanctioned picture. "They're going to need the energy," he added.

Kimberly smiled, but couldn't shake the feeling that she was in trouble, or, at the very least, that Daddy Teeks had lost some trust in her.

Chapter Thirteen

The campgrounds were—Clarissa had to admit—beautiful. The land featured tall, almost primordial trees and rolling wooded hills wherever the horizon was visible.

Every summer camp she'd ever seen on-set or on-screen had always been a chintzy New Jersey suburb affair. The kids in the middle of the country didn't know how great they had it.

She was beginning to turn the corner on this whole weekend, to feel like she could treat it like a mini-vacation, but that was before the first group of attendees arrived and spoiled everything.

Clarissa had meant to shower, she really had. After breakfast in the warm mess hall, her armpits were moist and her legs had gone a day or two more than they usually did without a shave.

But she'd gotten caught up at the lake.

Most of them had. Ivan Butinelli seemed to have no problem stripping off his shirt and laying out on the beach. Not the way an exhibitionist might, but more the way a dumb animal will sun itself on a rock, regardless to whether the warmth will expose it to predators.

Gina Bright also shed some of her clothing, but through some mishap she'd lain face down on the sand, one and only one bra cup still attached to her chest.

Clarissa caught Ivan looking, but noticed that he didn't let his gaze linger. Then she remembered back to that convention several months ago, to the way she'd seen the two acting, and figured that Ivan had seen the whole show at least once or twice.

Margery... Margery ...shit. Clarissa couldn't remember the old woman's full name. And she was the only one of the group Clarissa ever had any professional interaction with, but their time on set together hadn't been pleasant. Also not particularly memorable for the other woman, it would seem. They'd spent half a summer in Vancouver three years ago and still Margery hadn't shown the faintest glimpse of recognition when Clarissa had re-introduced herself to her fellow actor. If Clarissa weren't sure the woman hadn't become so indifferent to work, she would have taken the insult as a sign of a deteriorating memory instead of just an insult.

The old woman had moved herself into the shade of the stacked and covered tower of canoes, dusting off a rickety lawn chair and lowering herself down, ignoring Clarissa's offer of help.

"Old woman," jeez, Clarissa shouldn't be thinking of the other actress in those terms. If Margery weren't here, then *she'd* be the old woman. Gina Bright may have looked a similar age, but that was because of the hard mileage she'd drank onto her body, Clarissa knew the woman was only a couple of years over forty.

Of the group, only Marcus Lang and Tamara Reyes hadn't lingered at the lake and attached beach. Marcus had excused himself to make some calls while Tammy was busy receiving some kind of lecture from management.

Reyes seemed nice enough, if a little over-eager, but Clarissa caught the distinct vibe from Marcus that he thought he was above all of this. And he may have been right. All of them may have been above this. Clarissa certainly considered herself slumming, even if she did have less than five grand in her bank account. At least she was pretending otherwise.

Clarissa had her phone, but without any texts from Toby—she

assumed he would soon touchdown in L.A. and the torrent would recommence—she was able to sit on the end of the lake's small dock, put her feet in the water, and bliss out.

An hour or so got away from her and by the time she looked back toward the beach and the center of camp, all of her new friends were gone.

Gone and replaced with a few fresh arrivals.

Three men, one with a large camper's backpack complete with rolled sleeping bag and metal back brace, stood on the beach. The men were not grouped together like friends, but staggered.

It was involuntary, but Clarissa recoiled upon seeing them. Not simply because they'd surprised her, creeping up and replacing her fellow guests on the beach, but because they were all dressed the same. Dressed the same down to the fact that all three wore simple plastic masks.

They were masquerade masks without the sparkles or color, just white plastic with holes for eyes, nostrils and a small rectangular slit over the mouth.

The masks were the kind of Halloween costume preferred by teenagers who wanted to go door-to-door for candy and pranks, but didn't want to spend more than $1.50 at CVS to acquire their outfit.

"Hello," Clarissa said to the three.

She didn't get any response from the men outside of a slight head tilt from the kid wearing the pack. At least, she assumed he was a kid. He could have been anything south of 35. But he had the under-nourished body of a teenage horror nerd, so mask or no mask she would have always thought of him as a kid.

"You're all here for the con? What time is it?" she asked the boys.

Still no answer, but one of them turned and looked to the next closest one and shrugged.

Clarissa stooped and dusted off her ass with one hand while

picking up her sneakers and socks with the other. The wood of the pier had been mostly clean, but she must have rolled over onto some dried bird shit. Considering this, she kneeled and dipped her hand into the water to rinse. When she was done with that, she looked up again, their masks still impassive, their postures full of what they must have considered horror-movie menace.

"Very funny guys, but I'm not new to this you realize? I can't really be scared by this stuff, ya know?"

"It's, we're…" the kid carrying the pack started to say, his shoulders slumping. As he spoke one of the others shushed him, holding up a single finger to his angled plastic lips.

"Come on, guys. It hasn't even started yet," the kid with the backpack said to the other two. His voice was slightly muffled by the mask but he still spoke with an anxious teenager's rasp. He turned his attention back to Clarissa. "We're not supposed to talk to the celebrities. They gave us a whole lecture about it."

He made a frustrated groan and hooked a thumb under the bottom of his mask, stretching out the elastic string and giving his chin room to move. "Actually, we're not supposed to talk at all when we're wearing the masks," he said. "They said it's supposed to help with the immersion."

One of the other two men, still silent, crossed his arms and the other put his fists to his hips. They were staring daggers at the boy who'd spoken.

"Oh, okay. Makes, uh," she said, fighting to sound convincing, "some kind of sense."

She walked down the dock to shore, watching as the two closest to her alternated between watching her getting closer and continuing their angry stare-down at the kid with the backpack. The backpack and no willpower, apparently.

When one of them turned she could see that he had a paper

number pinned to the back of his shirt, the kind runners in a marathon get. So they could be identified by the con's organizers? Having your attendees be completely anonymous sounded like a recipe for disaster to Clarissa. Or were the numbers for when the field day games began? She was still unclear what exactly was going to go on this weekend. Would there be three-legged races and balancing eggs on spoons?

In addition to the number, all three wore the same mask, a set of colored plastic dog tags that must have been their lanyards for the con, and were identically dressed in jeans and plain black t-shirts.

It may have been October, but today was too warm to be in jeans. The ensemble may have been a uniform, but even if it wasn't, outside of camouflage cargo shorts the wardrobe of most con-goers was limited. That the T-shirts were plain, unadorned by gory images or reproduced poster art made Clarissa think that when attendees signed up for Blood Camp Con they were sent some kind of dress code. *Business casual, no open-toed shoes, a loaner serial killer mask can be provided upon request.*

The masks, the dance-troupe-esque uniforms for the audience, it reminded Clarissa of a show she'd seen on a trip to New York.

Sleep No More was as much a scene for Manhattan's hot young things as it was an off-Broadway show. An in-name-only "retelling" of *Macbeth*, the show was housed in a multi-level set designed to look like a 1920s hotel. The audience wore masks and were free to roam around the hotel grounds, following certain actors and storylines as the performers engaged in wordless dance/acting.

The show had been impressive, slick and sexy with just the right amount of pretentiousness to justify the ticket price. But even hiding her face behind a plastic *Eyes Wide Shut* mask, Clarissa had felt out of place among the drunken kids. The twenty and thirty somethings who comprised the audience were all marketing experts or "social media gurus" blowing off steam after a long not-really-work week.

Or maybe Clarissa would have had more fun if Toby hadn't insisted on coming along, wheezing into his mask after realizing that following the play's action required climbing a lot of stairs.

"Well, as you were then. Don't let me get you in trouble," Clarissa said to the kid with the backpack who'd helped her out by speaking up.

He just bowed his head to her as she past, getting back into character by silently reaffixing his mask.

The Three John Carpenter Amigos looked a bit silly in the broad daylight of late morning.

All of them left the beach when she did, following along as she joined the path back to camp and her cabin. She could hear their footfalls on the dirt and gravel behind her.

Okay. Maybe she was a professional at being stalked, but also maybe it was a bit unnerving, daylight or no.

Clarissa was used to conventions and overzealous fans that toed the line between enthusiast and stalker, but at those other cons there had always been plenty of witnesses and teams of security. At some of the bigger cons, promoters even had gone so far as assigning Clarissa a bodyguard detail of volunteers to walk her to and from her table and hotel room.

Here, out in the woods, she had none of that. The only thing she could rely on was that the expense of the event and seemingly strict rule set would keep her safe and keep the attendees well-behaved. Who knows how much they paid per ticket? Nobody was going to want to get thrown out on the first day. It would need to be Sunday that she worried about.

There was a slight mechanical whir somewhere above her and Clarissa scanned the tree line, spotting the tinted glass globe of a security camera. And there was *that* to keep her safe: she was being watched over by…someone. She'd only met Kimberly and Michael Teeks so far, but surely there were some more staff members she hadn't yet met working behind the scenes.

Her posse of observers grew as she passed through the center of camp, a few masked attendees who'd been milling around realizing that: *yo, that's Clarissa Lee.*

Antithetical as it seemed, it became easier to ignore them the more followers she gained and she stopped worrying entirely when the number of men trailing behind her topped out at seven.

In the distance, at the end of the packed-dirt turnaround that they'd driven in on, Kimberly had a card table set up under the camp's sign. Atop the table were stacks of white masks, piles of brochures, and a few boxes of ephemera.

At the side of the road, walking into camp, was a spotty procession of new attendees. All of them were wearing their jeans and plain black shirts, but none of them possessing a white mask yet. There were two girls in this group walking in, but outside of adding some gender diversity, their attire was identical to the males.

It wasn't even a full derisive joke, just the thesis that wormed its way into Clarissa's mind: something about how the two girls proved that being a horror fan was a learned trait, not an inherited one, because how could they make more with so few females? Eh, not her best.

Clarissa hadn't been paying close attention as Kimberly drove them in, but she couldn't remember seeing a parking lot further down that road, and it didn't seem plausible that Blood Camp Con was requiring its attendees to walk what had to be miles back from the main road.

As Clarissa watched, a school bus appeared at the end of the drive. It was a short bus, not one of the L.A. behemoths where every single kid seemed to be standing and yelling out the window when you passed them on the road. Probably couldn't hold more than twenty kids.

A couple dozen attendees filed off the bus and formed a line behind Kimberly's card table to get their goodies. Some of them looked in Clarissa's direction and pointed, but mostly they were fixated on signing in and receiving their masks, which they quickly donned.

Before Kimberly handed any of these materials over, she used a popsicle stick to poke around in everyone's overnight bags. It was the way some concert venues will check purses and backpacks under the auspices of security, but what they're really doing is making sure you aren't smuggling in your own bottle of water or package of Peanut M&Ms. Clarissa thought of the kid with the comically large backpack and how much Kimberly must have loved checking through that for any banned items.

Digging into her shorts pocket caused the fabric to agitate her skin and Clarissa realized she may have acquired a sunburn in October. There was nothing to be done about it now, she thought, and followed through with taking out her phone to check the time.

The opening ceremonies were scheduled to begin in fifteen minutes.

Not enough time to shower and barely enough time to throw on a new shirt and do her makeup.

While she had her phone out, she didn't notice that her reception had disappeared.

◆

It was only a slight rules violation. But Keith had to report it.

Definitely he had to report it. For sure. It could be a test. Somehow they would *know* if he didn't report it.

There was a clipboard to his right with a ballpoint pen attached to it by a bank chain. He checked the monitor and zoomed in with the trackball to make sure he had the camper's number correct. The guy had pinned his paper number to the canvas of his large backpack. Carrying the bag around seemed like a waste of energy when he could have just dropped it off at his bunk first. Who knows, if he'd stopped at his bunk first he probably wouldn't have made the violation in the first place.

There was no accounting for the decisions of an excitable young obsessive. As lame as it sounded: back in high school, Keith had never once visited his locker. It wasn't that he couldn't remember the combination or anything. He just *liked* keeping all of his books and assignments with him, in his Jansport. The extra strain on his lower back was a small price to pay for feeling as though he was ready for anything.

Oh well.

Keith copied down the kid's number, wincing against the raised flesh of the welt on his hand. The effort of messing up his face in response to his hand caused his nose to throb, a pain that radiated back to the rest of his skull, making the flesh of his ears feel hot. It was time to take more Advil.

Keith wrote: "Talking to CL" in the column next to the camper's number and returned the pen to its holster at the top of the metal clip.

"You got one already," Teeks said from behind him.

Either Michael Teeks was getting better at entering rooms or Keith's scabs had *again* covered his ear holes completely.

"Yes, I wrote down the number and type of infraction just like you asked," Keith said, finding his voice to talk to Teeks easier than he did with Rory, but not by much.

"Alright, thank you. Everything else good? Sound on the table mics is coming through clear?"

"Yes, Kimberly tested them earlier, the levels should be fine."

"Perfect! All you've got to do is keep everything in frame and hit Rory on the walkie when you get my signal. Everything else should be set it and forget it."

"I…um," Keith started, wanting to make a request but unsure

how to address Teeks for maximum servility. *Sir? Mr. Teeks?*

He didn't get to finish the thought.

"And, before we go any further, let me just say, Lumbra: you are doing excellent work so far. I know that Rory may... well I know that he may have an odd way of showing it, sometimes, but we're so happy to have you as part of the team."

This encouragement felt suspicious, but Keith wasn't sure quite why. He had done a good job in citing his first infraction. And Teeks was never the disciplinarian. The kind words emboldened him and he decided to spit it out: "Um, thank you. Mr. Teeks. But could I ask—"

"Ask away," Teeks said, not letting Keith finish. The ease of Teeks' manner made Keith almost certain that his boss knew what he was going to request and had decided to deny it ahead of the question being posed.

"Can I have some more Advil? My hand," Keith said, holding up where Rory had lashed him with the cable last night. It wasn't really his hand that hurt the worst, but Teeks needed Keith's hands to work the keyboard and mouse. "It's hard to, uh," he moved his finger in a clicking motion and made a show of wincing against the pain.

"Oh sure," Teeks said in a voice that said: *well duhhhh, I'm so forgetful.* He tapped his shirt pocket and the jingle of the pills inside their bottle hit Keith's blocked up ears like a cooling rain on a hot day.

Teeks squeezed open the child safety cap and rolled a single pill out into Keith's waiting, injured, hand.

The beige pill—small and round, the store's generic ibuprofen— looked like nothing in his palm.

"Can I maybe have two?" Keith asked, and felt the next words escape without thinking: "They're a very small dosage."

"Oh. Our first aid's not good enough for you, Mr. Goldman?" Teeks asked, then made to reach out for the lonely pill.

Keith closed his hand and scooped it into his mouth before even this tiniest of reliefs could be taken away from him.

"No no, it's enough," he said, trying to swallow the pill at the same time and almost coughing it back up.

When he was finished, Teeks spoke. "The pain keeps you sharp, Keith. Use it to do your job, do it well, and then we'll talk about whether or not you get any more of these." Teeks shook the bottle before returning it to his pocket. "Doesn't sound like there's many left, does it?"

Keith shook his head, unwilling to imagine how bad things would get if and when they did run out.

"Anyway. I've got to get out there. Good luck."

Keith swallowed again and still felt the pill. Without water it was stuck halfway down his throat.

"Oh and we should switch this on before we forget," Teeks said, leaning over Keith and turning the knob on the long box with the police antenna. It was a small motion on Teeks' part, but the man was demonstrating that he knew *exactly* what button presses would make the complicated console do what he needed it to do. Teeks didn't want to, but he could get along just fine without Keith Lumbra.

And that switch meant that any cell phone signal on campus should now be jammed.

Hopefully.

If Keith did his job right.

♦

"Look, yeah, we all love the movie, but I can't take a day out of my schedule to talk about it, on camera, *for free*," Marcus said into his phone. "This is my living we're talking about here."

This was beginning to feel like a waste. They were negotiating themselves around in circles.

The DVD market had been dying for years and, no matter what the nerd in your life told you: Blu-Ray was never going to take off in the same culture-shifting way. This meant that the major studios weren't dropping money on producing DVD extra features, commentaries, documentaries, like they used to, if at all. But in the last few years, several smaller distributors had moved in to take up the mantle and put out boutique re-issues of older titles. How these companies operated was to license limited home video rights from studios who could care less about a movie like *Town of Darkness*, which wasn't worth the effort of packaging and trying to sell to cable or streaming companies.

The distributors putting out these discs were small, so, while they would love to get as much of the film's still-living talent to talk about their experiences on camera (spouting bullshit like: "You wouldn't believe how much fun set was!", "He's a visionary!", and "Yes, we all still keep in touch!"), these small companies weren't normally willing or able to pay for it.

But, in Marcus' experience, they always offered participants some kind of honorarium for taking the time. That was, they offered the money eventually, if you kept stonewalling them and happened to be the star of the movie.

"And I understand your position," Marcus said, the heat of the sun on the tar-shingled roof of the cabin beginning to take its toll inside the small room. His tongue was drying up in his mouth and he kept looking at his watch. He could go for more of that grapefruit juice.

This phone call had taken longer than he'd anticipated and he was going to be expected at the opening ceremonies soon. "Believe me, I do feel for you, Cheryl, but I at least need to get beer money out of this. Don't say yes or no yet, just tell your team that's the way it's going to have to be for me."

There was a quiet on the other end of the line that was more absolute than the silent treatment.

"Hello? Cheryl?" Marcus asked into the phone.

There was no response. Did he just get hung up on by someone who had started out their conversation by asking him a huge favor?

He took the phone from his ear, stared at the screen, and tried redialing. Instead of a ringtone, he received an error message. Not low signal strength, but *no* signal at all.

Pacing between the bunks, going from Butinelli's side of the cabin to his own, Marcus caught a glimmer of movement at the window over the door.

"Can I help you?" he asked the masked figure that had his hand cupped over the glass. The man was peering in, using his hand to shield against glare like Marcus was some kind of peepshow performer.

The masked man didn't answer.

"Nobody wants to talk to me," Marcus grumbled to himself, returning the phone to his pocket and realizing that, come to think of it, the broken connection could work in his favor. Maybe by the time Cheryl from Graveside Productions was able to get back in touch, she'd be offering him a nice participation bonus in the *Town of Darkness* Twenty-Fifth Anniversary Edition Blu-Ray.

With the phone in his pocket and breakfast in his stomach, he was feeling good. Good enough that he wasn't going to take any shit from a creepy fan. It may have been twenty-five years since he was Sheriff Powers, but he was able to turn on his demon-killing *Walking Tall* shtick when he needed to.

"You don't want to talk, that's fine," he said to the man at the window and strode to the door. He stepped harder than he needed to and the heat-expanded boards of the cabin creaked under his feet.

As expected, the peeper retreated from his post.

Marcus opened the door, aiding his elbow with the end of his shoe, causing it to swing wide and slam against the frame.

The guy hadn't been alone. There were five more lookie-loos

outside the cabin, only the one had been brave enough to climb up and watch at the window. They flinched as a group when the door slammed, but, with an unspoken "safety in numbers" mentality they stood their ground.

Eh, what did it matter if they'd made it hard for him to concentrate on business. He was on their time now, technically, and felt ready to head to the opening ceremonies.

Only two more days of this shit, Marcus told himself. He shook his head at the gaggle of silent nerds watching him, one of them poking one of the others in the ribs and gesticulating.

Can you believe he's really here? he imagined he could read their thoughts.

No, he really couldn't believe it.

Chapter Fourteen

It was high noon above the stage at the center of camp and the audience looked...moist.

Actually, it was maybe twenty minutes after noon. The presentation had to be delayed to allow some campers to sign in and find a seat, but still the audience was damp.

There weren't many of them, forty, fifty at the most, but still the audience was a sea of white masks, oily hair, and pink forearms. The palest among them were already starting to redden up in the sun. Clarissa very much doubted any of these basement dwellers had the foresight to pack sun block.

There were no seats, but most of the audience was sitting anyway, crossing their legs and creating rows through sheer herd instinct. Those toward the back of the gathering chose to stand, towering above the groundlings. The ones standing with crossed arms were the most "alpha" looking of the attendees, the horror fans who were also weekend MMA competitors. Yes, there were in-shape nerds, if back alley crossfit and protein powder could be called fit.

"And finally, a woman who truly needs no introduction, but I'm going to give one anyway, Clarissa Lee, star of *Death Birth*, *The Rememberer*, *Nebula Journey*, and, my favorite: *Flag Day!*"

There was no curtain to walk through, so Clarissa stood by the side of the stage and waited for the fanfare to begin.

Having the event take place outdoors combined with the smaller size of the crowd meant that the applause was muted, at best. There were no hoots, only clammy hands colliding against one another.

Looking out at the masked faces, it was hard for Clarissa to tell if they were unenthusiastic or merely on the verge of heatstroke. She gave a slight bow before taking the fourth seat on the stage. There were two folding tables pushed together so the panelists had somewhere to lean and three microphones in small table stands. The remainder of the six seats had been grouped three and two to give the illusion that the fourth seat was the center of the panel.

Teeks was holding his own microphone. He'd already called the rest of her co-stars onto the stage and they'd taken up their places behind their cardboard nametags, each tag listing two credits, with Clarissa getting a whopping three. For someone who'd guaranteed them a unique convention experience, the first official event of Blood Camp Con was feeling awfully familiar. Clarissa had sat on hundreds of similar panels, over the years.

"Now, I know what you're thinking: you've seen this stuff before," Teeks said to the audience, miraculously guessing exactly what Clarissa had been thinking. "Or stuff like it. And while this is a fantastic lineup, it's not like you haven't met some of these people before, gotten their autographs even. This isn't our first rodeo, horrorhounds, am I right?" He paused for some kind of audience callback or laughter, but either they were stroking out or were still beholden to the no talking rule.

Teeks looked troubled, then snapped his fingers into the microphone and pointed to his temple to indicate that he'd just had an epiphany.

"I should clarify something: you can cheer and laugh and clap now. Even if you've got the mask on. This is a safe zone," he said, thinking of something. "And those front two rows?" Teeks said with a motivational speaker's conspiratorial chutzpah: "That is the splash zone. So are you ready for this weekend campers?"

There was a halfhearted cheer. With nothing specific to cheer at, that was to be expected, but Clarissa did see a few attendees lifting their masks, mopping their sweaty chins off on their black t-shirts.

"Hell yeah, Blood Camp Con!" Kimberly shouted, standing up toward the back of the mostly seated crowd, clapping. That did nothing to get them excited. If anything it had a dampening effect.

From Clarissa's vantage, so far this was a disaster.

Clarissa didn't have kids, but she'd been to enough dinner parties and barbecues to be familiar with the phenomenon of children wanting to "put on a show" for the adult guests. It was at times cute, but mostly Clarissa found the practice tiresome. Maybe it made her a bitter divorcée, but she didn't want to have to be polite and watch kids dance around, attempt a skit, and have none of their material land. The Blood Camp Con opening ceremonies were in the ballpark of that squirmy feeling, although Michael Teeks was a forty-plus-year-old man who'd spent tens of thousands of dollars to 'put on' his 'show.'

Everything about this presentation felt a little Neverland Ranch, and the embarrassment centers of Clarissa's brain twitched accordingly. She didn't particularly like the man, but she couldn't help but pity him.

"Now you've all signed off on your releases. And I see a lot of black t-shirts out there, which makes me think that you've read the rules completely, are in compliance of them, and are ready to have a fun weekend. So we don't need to get bogged down with going back over any of that, but the thing is," Teeks paused, standing at one corner of the stage, almost at the lip, and looking down the line of panelists.

Tamara Reyes was closest to him, then Butinelli, then Dame Margery, then Clarissa herself, then Marcus Lang, with Gina Bright providing the cap on the end. Gina checked her phone and looked confused at something she was reading onscreen. Her expression told everyone that she couldn't be bothered to listen to Teeks while something so puzzling was happening on her phone. *A drunk game of*

Candy Crush? Clarissa thought.

As she looked back over the guests, it didn't escape Clarissa that the arrangement was boy-girl. Nice one, Teeks. Very symmetrical.

"Our guests haven't been told the whole story." He laughed to himself, his affectation suddenly more southern gentleman, an amiable lay preacher. Clarissa felt her ears perk up at the mention of another surprise. "They've been told that they're going to have to do some acting this weekend. But they also need to know that there's going to be some cardio involved, too."

The crowd gave a gentle laugh in response. The laugh was low but more genuine than any of their feedback had been up to this point.

"When you arrived you were asked to fill out an elimination ballot," Teeks said, continuing to address his campers, "and I hope you turned that in to the lovely Kimberly when you were asked, because after this presentation is finished we will not be accepting them."

Teeks waved to Kimberly and she gave him a thumbs-up. Elimination ballot?

Clarissa was beginning to sweat, and not just from the heat, but at the mere mention of physical activity. Maybe she hadn't been that far off with her assessment of a field day. She tried to imagine what the splatterpunk version of a potato sack race would look like. But more importantly she began thinking of the most gracious way she could bow out before having to participate. What were they going to do? Demand that she gave her advance back? She was here and that should have been enough.

"And the guests of honor also don't know that there is *one more* special someone joining the camp this weekend," there was a hush over the crowd that was different from the silence that preceded it, and even Clarissa found herself hanging on Teeks' speech. "We promised you something unique, something revolutionary when we took your hard-earned money. And, friends: we intend to deliver."

Clarissa scanned the crowd again, wondering why the actors even had mics in front of them if this guy was just going to keep talking. But a curious shift had happened with the audience, the ones cross-legged on the grass and dirt were leaning forward and the ones standing had begun a subtle push in, the press of an outside concert crowd wanting to get closer to the music.

"We are creating a new icon here. A new legend of terror," Teeks said.

One audience member couldn't help himself, he didn't speak, per se, but he let out an "ohhhhh" and pointed to the stage, his finger just a hair away from pointing at Tamara Reyes, indicating the area above her.

"Ladies and gentlemen, I hope you've placed your bets, because The Fallen One has arrived at the first annual Blood Camp Con!"

Clarissa was able trace the line back from the audience member's finger and lean over the table just in time to see the large gloved hand close over Tamara Reyes's chin and pull her face up to the sky.

Someone had snuck onto the stage without them noticing, and that someone was now attacking the talent.

The girl let out a scream, a perfect scream. Jeez, maybe there was a basis for her precocious cult of fans. Some TV guest spots and only one feature film under her belt but still Reyes had pipes and could summon it cold, with no rehearsal. Clarissa was impressed, one scream queen to another.

Above Tammy stood "The Fallen One," and Clarissa's first reaction to him was:

Well, that's more like it. That *looks professional.*

The big man's costume was retro but fresh. Although the more she looked at it, the more she thought it was expensive-looking but maybe too ludicrous to "read" as menacing in the real world and in the harsh noontime sun. The character would look great on film, though.

The right director and editor could make any monster look good. On screen, you could hide it a bit more, control the points of focus, layer a character behind shadows.

Design-wise, The Fallen One was a heavy metal Jason Voorhees. He was a Cenobite by way of a Marvel superhero. The costume featured a weathered leather jacket that had dark, bony protrusions tearing through it at the elbows and shoulders. The big man wore a stylized demon-head mask that left a space for the actor's mouth and chin. It was a window of exposed skin that, while reminiscent of Batman's cowl, told the audience: yes, The Fallen One is supposed to be wearing a mask, not an actual demon.

The action figures would sell themselves.

And before Clarissa could even register that The Fallen One was brandishing a large chrome knife, he'd begun to run it across Tamara's waiting throat.

"What the fuck?" Ivan Butinelli asked no one in particular, leaning forward and blocking Clarissa's view of most of what was going on between Tamara and The Fallen One.

But that was fine, because Clarissa's eyes had followed the first trickle of blood as it became a foot-pumped geyser and sprayed out into the waiting crowd.

Oh. He'd been serious about the splash zone thing...

The first row of upturned faces transformed from white to red as the first pump hit them and then to pink as the splatter began to run off the slick plastic of the masks.

Everyone at the table pushed back their seats and lifted their arms away from the tabletop as the blood began to pool, the contours of the plastic tablecloth forming rivers and tributaries, but nobody stood up or tried to interfere with The Fallen One.

Maybe because they were all actors and had been around this kind of thing time and again: they knew that red food coloring left a terrible stain and that Caro Syrup quickly became sticky in the sun.

Or maybe it was because Tamara Reyes was better at screaming than she was at acting.

The girl kept her struggling and screaming going way too long after she should have quit and played dead. Theoretically, her vocal cords would have been severed, if the knife had gone as deep as it looked like it'd gone.

The Fallen One migrated his hand from Tammy's chin to the back of her neck and was pressing her face down onto the table while he continued to saw at her throat.

It was an odd memory to have at the moment, but Clarissa couldn't help but think of the game "Heads Down, Seven Up". Did elementary school kids still play that? The game was played by having a classroom of kids shutting their eyes and putting their heads down on their desks. Seven other students circulated throughout the room and selected their prey by pushing down the raised thumbs. The object of the game was to guess who chose you, if you were chosen.

It was an easy game to cheat at, of course. You needed to wrap your arms around your face but keep your eyes open to stare at the floor. When you got picked, you knew what kind of shoes your attacker was wearing.

Even with her head down, Tamara Reyes wasn't fooling anyone. If she had played "Heads Up, Seven Up" in school then she had probably been a cheater. And not a particularly subtle one. She was laughing as the tubing affixed to the latex prosthetic covering her neck started to sputter and run on empty. The mechanism shot out a mist of pink air in a dry whoopie cushion sound once its blood reserves were depleted.

Maybe Teeks saw or heard the actress' laughter, maybe he didn't, but he did speak up.

"Honored guests? Do you remember what I said about cardio?" He looked to the crowd. Most of them were standing at this point, their cheers much more authentic, then turned his attention back to the panel: "You all should be running right now. Or you'll be next."

Clarissa looked to Marcus Lang who then looked to Gina Bright. At least the other woman's phone was stowed away now, but she needed to stand up and get off the end of the stage if they were going to be able to flee The Fallen One the way that management wanted them too.

"Oh, okay," Bright said, nearly tripping over her own folding chair, but getting it together enough to run down the stairs. Clarissa hadn't seen her take a drink during the panel, but that didn't mean she hadn't been sneaky about the liquor she was keeping on her person. Or she'd snuck enough into her juice this morning.

It took the craziness surrounding them for Clarissa to pinpoint the exact reason she was uncomfortable palling around with Gina Bright. The (slightly) younger woman wasn't merely a "Clarissa Lee knock-off" as she wanted to think. No, Gina Bright *was* her. Bright was an alternate universe, through the looking glass, version of Clarissa Lee.

What if her divorce to Boyd Haight had come at a slightly different time in her life? Or what if Toby hadn't constantly been at her side at parties, asking how much she'd had to drink every time she returned to the bar?

Clarissa could have been Gina. And she could *still* be Margery, if she let herself get bitter enough. This wasn't a panel of experts, it was a gathering of Charles Dickens ghosts meant to scare Clarissa straight.

Gina climbed down the steps at the end of the stage and the rest of them followed. Margery was the only one of them who made no attempt to emote fear.

Teeks continued: "That's it, get out of here. I have no control over what The Fallen One does. Who would have thought that the young Ms. Reyes wouldn't have been our final girl?"

Clarissa and the rest of the group jogged to the path leading up to the cabins and stopped.

"What do we do now?" she asked her fellow guests.

"They could have given us a little direction," Butinelli said, frowning down at his shirt. "And a little warning. This is silk fer Christsake. Fucking ruined."

On stage, The Fallen One took his hands off Tammy and the actor playing him let out a roar and beat his empty hand against his chest, using the other to hold the knife aloft in a movie poster pose: *Star Wars, Conan the Barbarian*, take your pick of any poster featuring a magic sword and raised hands.

"The Fallen One, everybody. He'll be your slasher for the weekend," Teeks, said, applauding against the base of the microphone, causing noisy bursts of feedback.

There was a brief ovation and then Tamara Reyes *also* stood up and took a bow.

"Well, you're dead Ms. Reyes, but okay," Teeks said, his voice blurring the line between pretend annoyance and real annoyance. "And Tamara Reyes, folks. Ms. Reyes will be taking photos in the mess hall after we're through here. The same goes for all the guests who make it onto the elimination ballot."

The organizer of Blood Camp Con looked over to where Clarissa and the rest of the group were standing, then into the audience. "Kimberly, take care of them, please." He pointed to the clump of out-of-work actors.

Kimberly pushed through the crowd of standing fans. Before she was clear, she nearly tripped over backpack guy's pack, which he still hadn't stashed in his cabin, but was instead using as a seat. Kimberly jogged over to them while the action on stage waited, then resumed.

"Now," Teeks continued talking to the crowd, "before we get to the grub, let's do a quick rundown of what the rest of the weekend will look like…"

"I know this is a surprise," Kimberly said in a hushed voice, slightly out of breath from her cheering and running, but even more chipper than she'd been thus far. Which didn't seem possible. "But you are being paid to act. Try to think of the weekend like a big game of hide and seek or capture the flag. I'm not supposed to tell you where to go, but you do need to leave this area," she waited a beat and then added: "Please."

Clarissa looked to the rest of the group, Butinelli had been the one closest to Tamara when her "death" had come and he looked it. He'd tried to rub away the mist of fake blood on the side of his face, but his efforts had only succeeded in turning half his face rouge.

Marcus Lang was smiling, either a genuine smile or he was polite enough and a good enough actor to pull off sincerity.

Kimberly used both hands to shoo them away and they went, running to the safety of their cabins.

Meanwhile, on stage, Teeks kept talking.

Chapter Fifteen

Teeks' microphone was the only one of the four hooked into the loudspeakers.

Keith watched on the monitor as the man ran through a list of bogus events and rules. Even on the small, low-resolution screen, he could see Teeks' expression change as he looked off stage. He was making all of this up, killing time until something happened off screen.

Once the celebs had been chased away, Teeks dropped his mic. Keith could hear him talk through the computer speakers. The table mics ended up being more than sensitive enough to pick up his unamplified voice.

"Okay, they're gone. That's good. Now for a real show!"

There was a spattering of laughter, some of it uneasy and some of it striking Keith as *too easy*.

With that cue, Rory, as The Fallen One, latched onto Tamara Reyes. He caught the girl where the base of her skull met her spine and lifted the actress off her feet. It was amazing to watch an act of physical strength like that, knowing that there was no wire team on the other side of the stage helping augment the move. There were no special effects here.

How many times had Keith himself wanted to do something like this to one of his own actresses? The idea made him both nauseous and excited. How much of what he was feeling was exhaustion, infection, and dehydration and how much of it was a product of his warped mind?

Reyes screamed again, the sound somehow less intense now that the attack was real, like she was no longer playing it up. Rory dragged her over to the far end of the stage, away from where Teeks had set himself up.

The big man reared back and slammed Tamara's head against the folding table, her forehead connecting with the corner.

The top of her scalp and skull opened up and peeled back. The wound reminded Keith of the way a drunk guy might try to take the cap off a beer bottle without an opener, only to end up shattering the neck against a countertop.

A new wave of blood pushed across the tabletop, pushing the watery fake stuff out of the way in a darker gush.

"That's more like it," Teeks yelled and raised both his hands. The spectators visible on screen raised their arms in a similar "field goal!" gesture. The crowd went wild.

Once the show was over, Tamara Reyes' body slumping against the stage, the blood from her 'O' of an open mouth trickling to a drip, Teeks spoke again, his tone very matter of fact.

"Now let's eat and you guys can get those pictures taken."

◆

Kimberly depressed the shutter but wasn't happy with the results.

"Hold like that for a second longer," she said, showing the palm of her hand to the camper with his arm snaked around Tamara Reyes's shoulder. The young guy had his mask tipped up atop his head—the mess hall was considered a safe zone so he was allowed to remove it— and she could read the annoyance on his face.

The autofocus on the digital camera was killing her. She should have taken more time practicing with it.

She clicked again and the picture showed up on the small screen. It was still out of focus, but close enough to be serviceable. They couldn't all be perfect. She had a lot of pictures to take. Campers who completed the duration of the game, and paid extra for one of the photo packages, would be going home with a USB flashdrive with all their photos. Their numbers would help to identify them, sending them home with the right pictures even when they had their masks on.

"Next!" she called for another camper to take his place next to the corpse.

With no air conditioning in the mess hall and with the hot plates sitting out and open since this morning, the entire room felt and smelled like one big aluminum tray of scrambled eggs. Which was to say: humid and gross.

And now the room featured one dead body. One Twitter-famous corpse.

The next camper to take a seat next to Tamara Reyes also put his arm around her shoulder, but Kimberly didn't like where this kid chose to rest his hand.

"No, touching, please." Kimberly said.

The guy didn't respond verbally, but he did remove his hand, frowning as he did so. He turned to Tamara and mimed kissing her on her cold cheek, sure to keep a buffer inch between his lips and the dead girl's gore-streaked cheeks.

Even with only five seconds to observe him without his mask, Kimberly was able to write him off as one of those guys who was hyperaware of his masculinity. He probably bookmarked quite a few blogs about techniques for picking up women, but didn't go on many dates.

Before she clicked the shutter, Kimberly resigned herself to being perfectly okay if this guy's picture should happen to turn out shitty. Or maybe didn't make it onto his USB drive at all...

Kimberly was used to taking pictures on her phone, and was pretty good at it, too. Her iPhone's camera took higher resolution pics than this outdated Nikon. But, as Daddy Teeks had explained to her, even with network connectivity temporarily blocked, taking photos with a phone was too risky.

Apple collected so much data and the government just let them. Having a time-stamped, geo-synced, group of post-snuff photos stored in the cloud was too much of a risk. Even for MTY Productions, a company built on risk.

Planning for the weekend to start off with a scripted—a *fake*—death ran contrary to what they had conceived Blood Camp Con as being, but Daddy Teeks had made a compelling argument for it.

"I mean, I've never paid for a fight on pay-per-view, I'm simply not that into boxing. But I'm able to understand the disappointment that you'd feel if you paid, what? Sixty bucks for a fight? Only to have it end with a knockout in the second round.

"If we let the rest of the guests watch Rory make his first kill, his first *real* kill, they'll all scatter the second they see that what we're doing is real. Sure, that's going to have to happen eventually, they're going to have to be cued into what's going on. But if we start it this way then all the campers get to have lunch, get to have some time getting situated, and they're guaranteed more shocks distributed along an inflated timeline. There's no reason not to spread things out a bit.

"It's value-added. And then the rest of the game can start.

"We can tell Rory to make it look good, but who knows how long it's going to take? This is our first time doing it. It could all be over by the end of Friday. There are so many variables and we have a duty to give people a good show."

It may not have been every girl's idea of pillow talk, but that night it'd worked for Kimberly Yost. It felt good, actually, to problem solve and build in contingencies. Sure, they were trying to run Blood Camp Con like a business, but most of the money they were going to get from tickets would have to be put right back into the production.

Daddy Teeks had money, more money than anyone Kimberly knew, but that wasn't why she was attracted to him. She wasn't that kind of girl, a gold digger. Quite the opposite. The only thing that exhilarated Kimberly about her boyfriend's money was the almost recklessness with which he spent it. And he spent it on cool shit, too, not fancy cars. It was like he didn't care that he had it and didn't care if people knew he did, and wasn't worried if, one day, it had to run out. Money was just...vapor.

"I could drop dead tomorrow, then what good does it do me?" he would often say.

Kimberly took another picture, this camper choosing to stand behind Ms. Reyes' jaggedly lobotomized corpse. The guy looked pale, almost green. Kimberly would have warned him not to throw up on Ms. Reyes if she weren't so worried about embarrassing him into actually letting go of his lunch.

You're going to see worse, she thought. *You better keep it together, kid.*

Well, who was she to judge? It may not have been the gore at all that was making him feel peeky. It could have been bad eggs or the heat of the room. But still, there was an intriguing difference between the over-the-top sadism of something like the *Guinea Pig* films and seeing the real thing. No matter what a coked up Charlie Sheen will tell you.

She took the nauseous kid's picture and waved him away so he didn't vomit on the merchandise.

The change in the room happened so suddenly it took Kimberly a moment to notice. The mess hall's soundtrack of excited chatter and the scrape of plastic utensils on paper plates ended. The ambient noise was replaced with nervous, giddy, whispers.

"So damn cool," said the next camper in line to have her picture taken, sitting down next to the corpse.

The camper was a young girl whose uniform was slightly off-book. Her plain black t-shirt was a babydoll cut instead of the men's Fruit of the Loom stipulated by the rules. They'd put this rule in bold, under a header called "For Female Campers", but Kimberly doubted that infraction was going to be held against the girl. She remembered signing the female camper in without commenting on it. Sisters had to stick together, was the way Kimberly saw it. Some of the time.

Kimberly looked up from behind the Nikon's viewfinder to see that The Fallen One was now stalking through the mess hall.

"Someone must pay!" Rory yelled, not sounding like himself.

◆

The bodycam had been Keith Lumbra's suggestion, an attempt to keep himself useful once they'd arrived at the campgrounds and had begun the laborious processes of camera installation and set dressing. What camera angle was more *slasher* than a first-person POV?

His original idea had been to stitch a GoPro into The Fallen One's costume somewhere, but there was no way to configure those small cameras to broadcast their high def signal live into the studio.

Even as it was, the battery life on the bodycam (the same one that some police departments used) when it was broadcasting was prohibitive enough that Keith made sure not to radio Rory to turn it on until after the opening ceremonies. Keith had plenty of coverage out there, and The Fallen One's POV would be best utilized while he was out and about, stalking his prey.

The camera had been placed under the lapel of Rory's leather jacket, the lens not hidden in any way, but at least camouflaged by being placed in a sea of metal studs. They'd tried it in different locations but the camera needed to be high up and as near as it could get to

Rory's center mass to stop him from inadvertently eclipsing the shot by swinging his arms as he walked.

Keith watched the monitor as The Fallen One crossed the length of the mess hall, campers leaning away from him and scooting down on their benches as he approached. The view inspired the kind of motion sickness Lumbra experienced while drinking and trying to play video games at the same time.

Not only the vertigo, but the footage also created that weird sense of dislocation that only movies can. Objectively, Keith knew that he was only separated from the on-screen action by a single wall, but the fact that he was watching it on a TV meant that it felt like it had happened hundreds of miles away and years ago. About thirty years ago, if this was an honest to God slasher they were making.

The feed from the bodycam was coming in at a much lower bitrate than the wired input from the surveillance cameras, but the video quality wouldn't be as much of an issue as the sound. The microphone built into the bodycam scraped and popped with distortion every time Rory moved. Which meant that none of his dialogue would be unusable if he spoke it while walking.

"Someone must pay!" Rory yelled, clearly conscious of their sound restraints because he shouted it only after reaching the center of the room and coming to a full stop. It was silent around Rory, with a single awkward laugh from a camper who either couldn't cope with the fear or was genuinely unimpressed by how The Fallen One's voice sounded.

Keith had known that letting the slasher—*their* slasher—speak had been a bad idea. What movie did that? But Rory had insisted that he have "lines" when Teeks had pressed the issue. Keith wasn't going to weigh in as anti-talking slasher, of course.

"You," Rory said, pointing out with his left hand, the wide angle of the lens making the shot distort, giving Rory's arm a funhouse mirror's stoutness. The microphone then rippled, fabric rubbing against plastic, and the monitor went dark as Rory crossed his right arm over the lens. He was searching for something in his jacket and brought the hand back out with a small wooden carpenter's hammer, blunt on both sides.

With the body camera tilted slightly up, now that Rory was standing tall and pumping out his chest, Keith cycled through the two cameras in the mess hall to search for a better angle.

Rory had been singling out the camper with the oversized backpack and by the time Keith had been able to dial in the correct camera numbers, Rory had the kid's head locked under one of his big arms.

You did this, Keith thought to himself, remembering how he had written down the kid's number on the infraction sheet. But no, hadn't Teeks been standing right behind him anyway? *The backpacker did it to himself.*

"Please, I didn't do anything," the camper protested, but Rory ignored him, setting down the hammer on the lunch table to free up a hand. The camper hadn't been eating alone but the table was clear now. Most of his "new friends from camp" had left their trays.

The Fallen One undid the drawstrings on the camper's backpack with one hand and tipped the contents onto the mess hall floor. Keith spotted a can of Sterno, a change of clothes, bug spray, and a small tackle box. It was the kind of stuff you actually took camping. All of the items spilled out and scattered until the bag was empty. Or as empty as Rory could make it with one hand while keeping its owner in a headlock.

"Do. Not," Rory bellowed. He was sounding appropriately menacing, must have been getting the hang of his character's voice the more he used it.

Rory dropped the end of the bag and retrieved his hammer. Then he smacked the camper across the bridge of the nose with the blunt instrument and that ended his screaming.

Keith gave an involuntary hiss and his own busted nose stung in response and/or sympathy for that of the backpacker's.

"Do. Not. Talk." Rory let the guy's neck go and braced his arm between the table and bench. By aiming at the space where the kid's arm wasn't resting against the table, he was able to break the camper's wrist with another smack of the hammer.

"In."

He delivered another blow to the head as the camper tried to wave his unbroken arm out of range and the kid slumped to lay flat on the floor.

"No Talking Zones."

The Fallen One stamped down with a boot and whatever he'd done to the guy's legs and pelvis was hidden to all three cameras, but not the microphone. It was the sound of a head of cabbage placed under the back wheel of a golf cart. Don't ask how Keith knew that sound.

Teeks wanted the finished highlight reel to have a very naturalistic feel, but that didn't mean that turning up the broken bone sound in post would be lying. Keith made a note to do that later on, in editing.

After Rory had administered a couple more whacks, for which Lumbra switched to the bodycam on the main monitor, Rory dropped his hammer and started stuffing the camper into his own backpack.

He folded his extremities along their new joints and, surprisingly: it worked. The guy fit inside the pack.

No one cheered, and from what Keith could see, no one continued eating.

When Rory was finished wedging the camper into his own luggage, he took a seat at the empty table and waited there for a beat, breathing heavily.

Sitting and resting was an odd performance choice, but Keith had to respect it. And then he realized that he was being silly: Rory was a real dude, not an otherworldly embodiment of evil. He got tired and needed to rest, just like anyone else.

In the control room, Keith was hot and out of breath and all he was doing was sitting down. Assuming the heat wasn't a fever from his various infections, he could only imagine how sweaty Rory was getting inside his mask and jacket. They should have made the costume out of lighter weight material, but who knew it was going to be this warm in October?

Without a word, Rory stood and left the room through the double doors that led out to the rest of camp.

After thirty seconds or so of silence, the first of the campers pushed their masks back down over their faces and followed after him.

Lunchtime was over.

Chapter Sixteen

"Do you think she got paid the same amount as us?" Butinelli asked. "That's a bit part. Doesn't seem fair, if she's getting to go home after one night."

"No, you're right. It doesn't," Marcus said, not really agreeing, internally, but not wanting to encourage the continuation of a conversational loop they'd been stuck in for nearly an hour.

"So we keep waiting now? How do you think this works?" Clarissa Lee asked, standing from the edge of the bunk she'd been lying down on and joining the rest of them in the center of the room.

As much as Marcus tried to stay abreast of genre news so he could put on a good show for fans, horror movies weren't really his thing. But he did have to admit that there was so much junk that it made the quality material stand out, made it more easy to spot in a sea of dreck.

Not even a true horror fan, Marcus was nevertheless star-struck by meeting Clarissa Lee. How old was she? She couldn't be sixty yet, could she? Whatever her age, and he was aware of the cliché, that her age was merely a number. She looked good. Maybe not the teenager who'd made her name carrying Cthulhu's child. Or the twenty-something who had become her director/husband's muse-of-diminishing-returns in the late eighties. But Clarissa Lee was still a movie star, one whose beauty had entered a more earthy period. There was less gloss, less try-hard effort, to her body and face.

Marcus liked it.

When they were all done fiddling with their dead phones and having polite conversations about what the rest of their schedules for the year looked like, they came together in the center of the room to discuss what happened next. If not direct instruction from Teeks or Kimberly, at least an appearance from the camp's "slasher"—that big bastard—would let them know they were at least waiting in the right place.

They were currently standing in the girl's side of the cabin. The ladies had six bunks to Marcus and Butinelli's four, so their cordoned off section of the building offered a bit more room for air circulation. They kept the front door propped open, but still Marcus was looking forward to sunset in a few hours to cut the heat.

"Something better happen soon. It's too hot and it's getting dark," Gina said, peering out the nearest window between two bunks.

She was right about one thing: they'd been in the room almost an hour, waiting for some kind of indication of what to do next.

But it wasn't currently "getting dark" as she'd said. It was fall and the sun would be setting earlier in the day, but Gina Bright was wearing sunglasses inside. Nobody corrected her.

"Well, I'm not *running* anywhere," Margery Clampton said. As dismissive as the statement was, it was surprisingly cogent. Marcus took it as the first evidence they'd been given that the old woman was *at all* aware what was going on around her.

"Tammy clearly knew that her death scene was coming," Marcus said. "She had to go away with Teeks and get prepped with rigging, cues, and makeup. I know that *I* haven't had that kind of briefing. And I get the feeling that we're all currently waiting on whoever's supposed to die next."

Clarissa nodded at this. "So who is it? Let us know where we've got to be and when so the rest of us can relax."

Marcus looked to the faces around him. Margery shook her head, Ivan leaned his head against the closest top bunk and said "I wish I knew," and Gina was still watching out the window.

"Ms. Bright?" Marcus asked. She didn't answer him. "Gina?"

She turned to face the rest of them, realizing that she was being spoken to. "Oh, shit no. I'm not getting messy today, maybe Sunday morning," she said, then hooked a finger to the window. "There are, um, well there may be something happening now, though," she said, slurring only a little.

Marcus spotted the top of a camper's head approaching the open door to the cabin. The kid took a timid step up onto the porch so he could peer over the threshold and into the cabin.

Around them, the room seemed to darken slightly, either a shift in cloud cover or...

Faces pressed against the room's four windows, campers going to tippy-toes and pressing their masks to the sills in order to watch inside the room.

Marcus, a man who'd been on sets where there were upwards of thirty people behind the camera, had never felt more on stage. No, not on stage, because he wasn't performing. This instead must be what a wild animal feels in a zoo. He and his fellow guests were in a fish bowl.

"I guess lunch is over," Butinelli said. It was strange that he really talked like that, in semi-one liners. What unseen camera crew and director was the Russian playing to? Or was he a method actor? Either way, it was surprising that he didn't have a bigger career. Or a bigger career where he got to keep his pants on.

Clarissa shushed him.

"Listen," she said.

They all did. Even Gina got her drunken labored breath under control long enough for Marcus to hear what Clarissa had been pointing out.

"An engine?" he asked.

The sound was getting closer, coming around the back of the building, through the side of the partition that led to the boy's quarter of the cabin.

"Are there motor boats on the lake?" Butinelli asked.

"No. I didn't see any. And how can *you* not recognize that sound," Clarissa said. Marcus had trouble placing it until she chastised the other man for it.

"That's a chainsaw," Marcus said, suddenly feeling more alert in the hazy afternoon.

Clarissa gave him a look and a condescending half-smile that said: *You get an 'A' for the day!*

Even when she was tossing sarcasm at him, he chose to see the playfulness in it: choosing to imagine the possibility of maybe hanging out sometime later this weekend. A private hang out session.

The sound of the idling chainsaw came closer, stopped, and then filled the room as the door on the other side of the partition was swinging open.

"So we run?" Marcus asked while looking around, still unsure how this game they were in was supposed to be played. He wondered which of them was supposed to be the next to go, whether anyone knew but wasn't saying. The actors had no reason to lie to each other. But they *could* be lying, and if Marcus was going to put money on which of the other actors had a secret meeting with Teeks to plan their death, his bet would be either Gina or Ivan.

But he'd been the one on his phone before the ceremonies, sequestered in the cabin and trying to negotiate his deal with Graveside Productions. It was very possible that Marcus himself was everyone else's chief suspect.

There was the creaking of floorboards as the chug of the motor came closer to the partition. The wall was a simple canvas tarp that had been staple-gunned to the floor and ceiling to divide the rooms.

"Let's get out of here," Marcus said again, the other actors simply standing and watching the not-a-wall. He couldn't tell if his nerves were the feeling that a loud rolling noise provoked, or whether he was just anxious to perform without a script or clear direction.

Outside the open door, he could see that there was a bigger crowd of masks jockeying for position. Marcus wondered, if he did flee, if the bystanders would be quick to move out of the way if he or his fellow actors would need to push through. It would be against the rules for them to interfere, wouldn't it?

"Yeah, let's do it. The beach is probably still nice," Clarissa said. She was trying to sound calm, but it was clear that not even the most experienced horror actor among them was immune to the chainsaw jitters.

Marcus had seen this phenomenon before. It had been on one of the two occasions he'd been a guest at the opening of a haunted attraction. Presiding over one was kind of their cottage industry's equivalent of cutting the ribbon at a supermarket opening.

Even though attendees at these things knew the chainsaws were fake—or had at least been made safe by removing the chain and getting a soft rubber bumper placed over the blade—there was something about the rumble that made the caveman part of one's brain reject rational thought. That was why every haunted house worth their salt had at least one guy with a chainless chainsaw stalking the grounds. The tools were great for crowd control and mood setting. There was something visceral about that sound, the way the vibration stuck in your chest.

They listened as the chug of the idling chainsaw reached the middle of the room, as close as it could get to the partition, and then revved, causing all of them to move for the door at once.

All of them except Margery Clampton. The old woman had

flinched like the rest of them, but kept both feet planted to the floor, watching the partition. Ms. Clampton was doubling-down on her vow that she would not be running anywhere.

The rest of the guests took a step and stopped as one. Marcus looked back and watched as the familiar, phallic, end of the chainsaw appear in the canvas. The blade split a slash into the partition. Chunks of fabric and a cloud of dust spewed out from the whirring chain. The chain that was still attached to the end of the chainsaw even though there were actors in this room. The insurance liability would've been enough to make Marcus's head spin if he weren't so intent on watching where that chain was headed.

Almost instantly, the hole in the divider became a chimney, filling the ladies' side of the cabin with gasoline exhaust. Apparently, with all that standing he did on the other side of the room, The Fallen One had hotboxed his portion of the cabin.

"It's a real fucking chainsaw," Butinelli said, the first of them to be able to speak and resume his progress out the door.

Everyone moved back except Margery Clampton, who crossed her arms in defiance to both the noise and smell.

The teeth of the chainsaw continued whirring. On the other end of the divider, The Fallen One pushed the end of the blade so far down to the bottom of the canvas that it nicked the floorboards and sputtered sawdust into the air.

The opening into the other room was now wide enough that the biker-cum-slasher was visible beyond the old woman, his bulk outlining her lighter dress with his black leather and chrome.

"Come on," Marcus said to Margery, not sure if he was being stupid and asking a trained actress to abandon her pre-assigned cue. Had she been playing all of them? By refusing to leave this mark was she just performing her part, as scripted?

With one bone-spurred forearm, The Fallen One spread the

curtain wider and stepped into the room.

"I'm done with this shit," Margery said to him, craning her head to look the tall man in the face. His eyes were ringed with black grease-paint to make it harder to tell where the man's flesh began and his mask ended. He let the chainsaw idle and stood stock still, pressing out his chest as if he were allowing Margery to sniff an invisible flower on his lapel.

"It didn't used to be this way," Margery continued, her thoughts seeming rushed but her voice articulate and sharp. "Men were men and women were dames and the movies *meant something*. And the movies that *didn't* mean something were disposable garbage for kids and we all acknowledged that. We knew what junk was! It wasn't meant to last!"

The Fallen One gave her a slight nod—respect? Grudging acknowledgement?—and then lowered the chainsaw into her collarbone. The weapon was very real.

There was no way to fake what came next.

Chapter Seventeen

Women and children first was *so* last century.

At least this was what Ivan Butinelli thought to himself as he was first out the door. He hadn't pushed anyone out of his way or trampled on any pregnant ladies or anything, but he hadn't encouraged any of the three women to get out of the cabin ahead of him.

There was no way he was standing around and huffing gasoline fumes while some redneck swung heavy machinery around inside of a tight space.

His right to escape without fear of offending other ages or genders was what equality was all about, right?

He looked back, watching through the doorframe like he was one of the spectators, one of those dopey kids in white masks.

As for the old lady...

From where he was standing, on the patch of dead grass a few feet out from the cabin's stoop, he couldn't see much.

But what he could see from his vantage didn't seem like a special effect.

Or, maybe it *did* seem like a special effect but not one that could be achieved in-camera, with puppetry and silicone. There would definitely need to be some CGI and green screen involved.

Shit, most of the fuck scenes he performed on a daily basis required more movie magic, cutting the camera, pausing a contiguous sequence to drink lots of fluids to wash down his pills. Recently there had even been one or two stunt cocks spliced in from the production company's vast library. He wasn't proud.

No, the old lady split in two, no VFX team needed. She was a grouchy old amoeba that had finally had enough and was divorcing its top from its bottom half. The split happened diagonally, from her right shoulder down to her left hip.

For a moment the two slices of her wobbled in the air against the tug of the chain and then slowly began to split in opposite directions. Her head fell back towards the open door while her right shoulder and arm fell down and forward, towards her attacker.

The two younger women—young*er* but not young, he'd realized that fact upon seeing Gina Bright again, a few months after their ill-advised hook up—spilled out of the room next and obscured his view for a moment, followed shortly by the black guy, Marcus. Only he wasn't so black anymore, and not nearly as collected as he'd been when he was lecturing them all in the cabin.

Marcus Lang was covered in blood, the front of his shirt no longer white, but pink where it hung loose and dark red where it was saturated enough to suck against his skin.

And Ivan thought he'd gotten it bad with the *fake* blood. That had been nothing, and at least he'd been able to change out of his ruined silk shirt. It was too hot for the long sleeves anyway.

What was he thinking? Was he entering some kind of shock? This was an emergency...

"It's real!" Marcus yelled, echoing Ivan's thoughts. "Someone get help!"

None of the bystanders looked like they were running to get help. They just pushed in towards the action and craned their necks to get a better look, careful not to bump into Ivan or the rest of the guests.

Marcus Lang put an arm on each of the women and pushed

them away from the door, the same way you would clear the area of a burning building if you were worried the windows were going to explode outwards, showering everyone in glass.

Ivan didn't follow after them. Instead he stayed to watch the old woman and the big guy. The chainsaw had reached her hip and stopped, the blade getting caught against the bone and grinding to a halt.

She was old, it was completely possible that she'd undergone hip replacement surgery. They made those things out of titanium. Ivan knew this stuff because he'd needed to visit a specialist himself, after his weekly visits to the chiropractor had stopped helping. Having his back cracked had actually started making his post-work aches and pains hurt worse, his bones letting out louder pops every time. But there was nothing, or nothing his insurance would cover, that the specialist could do for him.

As if to confirm this bionic-hip theory, the chainsaw whirled briefly and stopped again, gears grinding and plumes of black smoke making it harder to see into the room.

Letting the chain idle instead of doing any further damage to the tool, the big guy, The Fallen One, howled out an expression of frustration against the fact that his weapon was now fused into the old bat's pelvis.

Even in death, Margery Clampton was making life more miserable for those around her.

The big man took a few steps toward the fresh air and the observers who'd pressed in for a better look gave him a few feet wider berth. The Fallen One kept a hold on the chainsaw's crossbar with one hand and dragged the two halves of Margery Clampton's corpse behind him. She left two distinct blood trails across the floorboards.

"Whoa, awesome," someone next to Ivan said under their breath. It was one of the "campers," and the kid took a step toward the door where his buddies were beginning to form a barrier.

Ghouls, all of them.

Indignance wasn't something Ivan Butinelli allowed himself to engage in often. He'd seen enough holier-than-thou finger wagging leveled at people in the porn industry. He didn't judge often because he didn't like being judged. And, if he was being honest, he had a fairly deep reservoir of shame as it was.

Ivan was a guy in porn, and an old school one at that. If he were a female performer he could have been one of those alt-girls who wrote, directed and produced their own scenes. Those girls tried to put the onus and agency onto themselves, and were applauded for it. If Ivan were a younger man, he could at least be an "ally".

But he was older and old school. When he started in the biz he was dumb and coked-up enough that he hadn't even realized he was supposed to adopt a cute stage name, he'd simply shifted his middle name (inexplicably Italian) over to make a new last name.

His reluctance towards flying into an indignant rage wasn't because he *couldn't*. No, he was *very* good at indignant raging, but that temper was part of what had gotten him exiled from "legitimate" film work, so he'd been making a conscious effort to curb it in recent years.

But hearing the geek in the mask marvel at a little old lady being chainsawed in half made him angry. It made Ivan Butinelli righteously angry.

"You think that's cool?" Ivan said, coming up behind the kid. He put two hands flat on the attendee's bony shoulders and pushed. For someone who was in the same size and weight class as Ivan, the shove would have simply staggered them, but it sent this scrawny kid to the ground.

In the air, the spaz was barely able to get an arm out in front of himself. He skidded one elbow against the gravel and dry grass and Ivan could see that the skin there was already all torn up and gritty.

"Mother fucker," Ivan said and used one toe to tap the kid in the gut. It was not a real break-your-ribs kick: just a tap, really.

"Ivan, leave it, we've got to go!" Marcus shouted to him. Ivan glanced up to see that Marcus and the others were at the edge of the woods, the three other pseudo-celebrities were far away from the action, huddled together in the brush but still visible.

Ivan ignored him.

The kid on the ground was holding his stomach with one hand and picking dirt out of the abrasion on his elbow with the other. It was hard to tell with the mask, but it sounded like he was crying.

"You like seeing people hurt but you can't take being pushed? Fucking pathetic fucking loser. Impotent nerd." Even though he was the one who said it, the word 'impotent' still caused Ivan to get an involuntary shiver at the base of his neck.

No, never impotent. I'm good to go whenever and wherever, just get those lights set up.

Instead of making real contact with the kid, he kicked again and stopped short. His shoe scuffed a cloud of dust and sand into the wound that the kid was trying to clean.

Made you flinch. He'd never been one of those guys growing up. He'd been self-conscious about his accent, but, even still he'd been big enough to be invited to hang out with *those guys*. No, he'd hadn't taken them up on that, had never become a bully, but, then again, he'd never been on the receiving end of a push into a locker. So how could he empathize?

"Stop it," someone said. Ivan looked up in time to see a camper covering her own mouth, like she'd caught herself talking when she wasn't supposed to be. They took the rules seriously around here, even when one of them was being assaulted.

The female camper was a tad overweight, but these days who wasn't? She was a *shapely* girl. What was she doing out in the woods blending into this malnourished sea of paleness and bad skin? That's what he would have asked her, had he not realized that every single white mask in camp was now turned towards him. There was no expression on their plastic faces, but he could sense the anger rolling off of their postures.

Him beating up one of their own had become the main event and even The Fallen One had leaned against the cabin's doorframe, watching Ivan with crossed arms.

"This is insane. Somebody call the cops!" Ivan said, then pointed to the goon in the leather jacket and the heavy duty mask. "That guy should be in fucking prison."

He didn't know where he was going with this line of reasoning, because clearly something was not right and no cops were forthcoming.

Then the laughter began.

The sound seemed to roll forward, starting at the furthest row of campers, the ones still arrayed around the cabin's windows, and not petering out until it reached the front half-circle where the lone fangirl was standing.

And the laughter ended with the kid, still parked on his ass at Ivan's feet, his white face pointed now so that Ivan could see that his eyes were red and that the little pussy *had* been crying.

Being laughed at was certainly a trigger for Ivan's indignant rage, the aspect of himself fueled by the volcanic rolling of that deep well of shame he kept covered.

Ivan curled his hand into a fist, remembered to press his thumbprint flat against the knuckle of his pointer finger, bent slightly at the waist so he had a straight shot, and then let loose, punching the prone kid in the mouth. There was no holding back, not like he'd done with the kick.

Lashing out wasn't going to help anything about the situation, but it felt good and it had been a while.

The nose of the kid's mask crumpled inward and as Ivan pulled his fist away the plastic stuck to the sweat on his knuckles. The elastic strap stretched and then snapped the mask back onto the kid's face. The mask dangled, the holes crooked over his eyes.

It was probably only a second, but it felt longer, until a single trickle of blood leaked out of the rectangular mouth and the kid fell onto his back. Knocked the fuck out.

There was silence and heavy breathing for a moment. With the slight breeze, it wasn't as hot as it had been inside the cabin, but still Ivan was sweating.

The first thrown rock didn't connect. It didn't even come close, touching down three feet in front of both of them, leaving a divot in the soft ground and then bouncing to a stop against the dazed kid's leg.

Ivan looked up in time to see a second stone coming towards him and he moved so it didn't strike him.

The geeks were tossing rocks at him, a herd of water buffalo protecting their own and getting violent even when it didn't seem to suit their nature.

Wanting to keep an eye on the real threat, Ivan focused on the top of the stairs. The summer camp psychopath, The Fallen One, was still there. The big man had his arms crossed and had left his chainsaw (and the bifurcated monster movie starlet) abandoned in the room behind him.

The third rock connected. It had been thrown in such an extreme Hail Mary arc that even while Ivan watched it leave the hand of a beefy camper at the back of the ranks, he hadn't been able to track its trajectory against the orange afternoon sun.

The rock was maybe the size of a baseball and it clipped the left corner of Ivan's forehead and ricocheted off at an angle. Ivan felt the vibration of the hit in his teeth and his vision dimmed, then just as suddenly went bright, like someone putting their hand over a light bulb but quickly retreating from the heat.

Fine. He was fine. He lifted his hands up to defend himself from any more projectiles.

"Throw another one, go 'head," he yelled and found himself stepping towards the group of campers. "Come on, you dickless wonders." He glanced over to watch Marcus start to run over to his aide but the man was held back by Clarissa Lee. That was smart of her. Any more of them got in one place and that big fucker's job would have been made far too easy.

"Let's go," she mouthed to Ivan's bunkmate. Yeah, he couldn't blame her. This wasn't going to end well.

The campers shared some looks between them, wordlessly conferring, and then The Fallen One spoke up.

"Did you hear what he called you?" he asked, projecting the question over the crowd. The guy was putting on some kind of voice, some mishmash of a British accent, a southern accent, and a speech impediment.

The campers didn't seem to mind how ridiculous he sounded, never mind how ridiculous he looked in that outfit. Which didn't surprise Ivan. Nerds liked their villains heightened. As long as something had the outer veneer of being dark and self-serious, its core could be as silly as it wanted.

Ivan looked behind him, where he'd assumed would be nothing but empty field and the rest of the camp's structures. Only now there were a dozen or so campers gathered in the clearing behind him. Either they'd deliberately flanked him or all these new campers had been Johnny-come-latelys.

"Kill him, friends," The Fallen One bellowed.

Ivan put up his fists and they began to close in.

Chapter Eighteen

"That was unexpected," Teeks said, standing over Keith Lumbra's shoulder.

Keith didn't know which action he was supposed to be following on the main screen: there was the fleeing group, headed up by Marcus Lang—not a final girl, but that was fine, Teeks had assured him—or the fans beating Ivan Butinelli to a bloody pulp.

From the camera atop Deer Cabin, there was a good aerial shot of the circle of bodies that had formed around Butinelli. Making an executive decision, he held on that, making sure to follow the three others with the secondary monitors. Keith had been prepared for the possibility of the guests not sticking together and scattering into the woods. In that case, he would have had to choose a favorite, anticipating the ones Rory seemed most likely to follow and attempt to keep radio contact with their slasher. Now, having only two groups to worry about had actually streamlined things.

"It's not how it's supposed to go! It's wrong," Kimberly said from the back of the room. Her voice was stopping just short of a child's whine.

Before she'd piped up, Keith had almost forgotten the girl was there. He'd spent so much time in captivity with Rory, and even then there'd been only occasional appearances from Teeks. The introduction of a third person to keep track of and fear meant that he'd refused to believe Kimberly was anything more than a muffled voice on incoming calls. That she would turn out to be the youngest of the four of them had been a surprise, and *how young* had been an even greater surprise. She looked like a high schooler, a freshman co-ed at a community college at the oldest.

Over the phone she had seemed to fill the role of the head of consumer relations, interfacing with fans and fielding questions about the event and ticket prices. Teeks had also called her up when he'd needed a general problem solver when it seemed like Rory couldn't handle a task. Which meant that, once he'd seen and heard her in real life, he hadn't anticipated there'd be this much whining.

"It may not be what we planned, baby. But it's still something," Teeks said, sounding like he was trying to placate his young ingénue. "It really is something to see."

Whether the campers were choosing to fight Ivan Butinelli this way because they were frightened or because it was the way that fights happened in movies, Keith could only guess. If they would all rush the porn star at the same time, the brawl would be over in seconds. But as it was, they'd formed a ring around the man, with only two of the crowd brave enough to step forward and start swinging.

There were two prone bodies inside the circle now, the original camper that Butinelli had sucker punched and a second, bigger dude who had walked right into the porn star's elbow upon entering the ring. Bravery was no match for bloodlust with what looked like a little bit of training behind it.

"Oof," Teeks said, responding to something onscreen. A chubby guy had knit his fingers together and was slamming both hands into Butinelli's back. It was a move that Keith had seen on pro wrestling and it probably wasn't practical in a real fight because the camper jumped back, shaking out both hands, jerking his fingers in pain. Butinelli seemed unharmed by the attack.

"Can you zoom in?" Teeks leaned in and tapped the screen.

Instead of losing the panorama of action, Keith obeyed Teeks but kept the movement to a very slight, steady zoom. Too fast and the transitioning footage would be unusable. He eased his finger a millimeter forward on the trackball. He was technically listening to his boss—how he'd come to think of Teeks—but wasn't going too tight on the action.

Asking for the zoom was either the manifestation of true producer's instinct or a lucky guess on Teeks' part. The tide of the action took a decided turn in favor of the campers and the camera was now close enough to catch all the details:

One of the brawlers scooped up one of the thrown stones from earlier and smashed it across Ivan Butinelli's face. The shot was tight enough that they caught the shadow of blood leaving Butinelli's mouth and landing on the dead grass by his feet.

"It's not right. They're all breaking the rules! They're supposed to be melding into the background. The campers should be an invisible sea of faces," Kimberly said. She was fully whining now, a panicked tantrum.

And he thought *Teeks* had been the control freak. This girl wanted everything scripted, even the uncontrollable actions of the fans.

You mean their insane, spectator-sport murder game wasn't unfolding exactly how they'd planned it would? Shocking!

In his old life, the one in which he'd been spilling fake blood and (mostly) fake puke to make his own movies, Keith had hated people like Kimberly. They were the ones that didn't see what the big deal was about getting a production to work just the way you wanted it to, the ones that couldn't grasp that a production schedule needed to be a fluid thing. These kinds of people were poison on set. They were always full of questions ("How is this going to cut together?" and "Why are we doing this?") and constantly complained when days went overtime or more than two takes were needed.

He especially hated the *women* who acted like this. They couldn't see the art in the struggle and would never get it. But that wasn't something you could say on the internet without the P.C. Police labeling you a misogynist. Which maybe he was a touch, but still.

"This footage is great," Keith said, trying to present a rebuttal to Kimberly, however minor. He didn't turn back to face her. He tried to say it more to the room in general, if that was possible.

He regretted the attempt.

Teeks gripped the back of Keith's roll chair and swiveled him halfway around so he could still keep a hand on the trackball.

"Do you have everything all set for a moment so I can tell you something?" Teeks asked, raising his eyebrows like he was talking to a child.

At his ankle, Keith felt the tug of the bike lock. There was some wiggle room there, if he laid flat on the ground and was able to get his shoe off, it was possible he could work the chain off without having to saw through his foot. But that would require some real mobility, and his sore body wasn't exactly feeling up to yoga.

Escape was off the table, probably.

Keith said that, yes, he had everything set with the feeds for a minute. Teeks' face was so close to his own that the pulse of the man's breath was making the open skin of Keith's nose buzz.

"*She*," Teeks pointed a finger over to Kimberly, "is just as important a contributor to this project as I am. *She* is merely concerned that the event runs smoothly, which is *her* job. *You*, Lumbra, Goldman, whoever you are," he turned the finger back to Keith and let it hover, millimeters away from the end of his nose, "You are a contractor. You don't get to editorialize. Is that clear?"

"Yes. I'm sorry," Keith said, and he was.

"That's good, back to work," Teeks said, and flicked the end of

Keith's nose. From Keith's cross-eyed vantage it hadn't looked like much of a flick, more of a lazy afterthought than a vicious attack, but it hurt so bad he thought he was going to pass out.

In the corner, somewhere out of sight, Kimberly laughed.

He hated them all, but somehow, even though she hadn't been the one beating him and starving him, he hated the bitch the worst.

"Don't worry, baby. I'll call up Rory and get him back on point," Teeks said.

Chapter Nineteen

"There's a gun. Back in my cabin. And I think it's real, and I think there are bullets for it, too," Clarissa said and immediately she could see Marcus's features crush together into an expression of skepticism. They were handsome features, but when they looked like they weren't taking her seriously she wanted to smack them, to rearrange them on his face.

"They've got to know about it, right?" Marcus asked. "Why would they let you have a gun?"

"God, we need to go," Gina Bright said, interrupting. She didn't add anything to the conversation except a whiff of halitosis. Clarissa could see herself in the woman's dark sunglasses. She'd looked better, but at least she wasn't in the middle of a lifelong bender.

They were all crouched and whispering. Stage whispering, more like it. There weren't any campers paying attention to them anymore, the attendees all busy as they were converging on Ivan.

Inside the circle, catching glimpses of him from around the shoulders of campers, the man had both fists raised and was bouncing on the balls of his feet like a boxer.

Butinelli was nearly as old as she was, but he'd clearly kept in good shape. Under his leathery skin were knots of muscles that had grown prominent now that he was flexing and glistening on this unseasonably warm afternoon.

"They called it a game," Clarissa said, trying to remember how she could make her case. "Teeks and Kimberly, they called it that. Maybe it really is one and maybe they've set it up so it's halfway fair. They could be letting us arm ourselves."

"Or they want to keep us in this place long enough for that guy to come after us," Marcus countered, hiking a thumb toward The Fallen One. "It's not like they have the whole camp fenced in. If we run into the woods, and try to stay headed in the general direction of the road, we can make it out."

What made her angriest about the way he was delivering his argument was how much sense it made. Who knew, she could go back to her cabin and find that the gun was gone, a prop that had been struck while they were at the opening ceremonies. Or it could be just that: a prop gun that shoots out a white and red "Bang!" flag when you pulled the trigger.

Or she could be right. There were ways to make escape difficult, fences and bear traps and who knew if they weren't being GPS tracked somehow. It was all enough to feed Clarissa's inner conspiracy theorist until she was overfull.

She looked back to the cabin. The Fallen One turned his head from the circle of fans beating on Ivan Butinelli back to where their group was crouched. They didn't have enough cover to be hidden. With the mask and the distance, there was no reading the giant's expression beyond the coy smile on his lips, but he seemed contented to watch from his perch.

"But it's a gun!" she yelled, finally, and clamped onto Gina Bright's hand. With Marcus's hand clasped in her other, she towed them behind her, headed off in the direction of her cabin.

Either she'd won Marcus over with her argumentative skills or he figured any progress was better than watching his bunkmate get torn apart by the most rabid of fanbases.

◆

"Fallen One? Come in?" Daddy Teeks said into the walkie-talkie. The plastic yellow and black walkies were old technology, the kind of thing that could be purchased at a Toys R Us, but they had a decent enough range to cover the camp and weren't tied in to a network like a cell phone would be.

It took a moment for Rory to respond. Kimberly watched on one of the smaller monitors as he retreated out of the doorway to the cabin, out of sight of the campers. This was a technique that they'd established. It was fine if the slasher talked, but he could not be seen answering to some kind of higher power. It would hurt the illusion for their paying customers.

Not that they weren't all giving rapt attention to the fight.

Things had gotten bloody now, even on the small TV she could tell that Butinelli's scalp was gushing. But things were looking up for the porn star: he'd managed to wrestle the stone away from his most recent attacker and was now crushing the other man's head with the rock, cracking open the plastic of his mask from nose to nostril.

It was unfortunate for repeat business, but that guy dying did mean there was one less DVD they would have to burn later and one more prize pack they would be able to relist on the web store.

"Yeah, I'm here, over," Rory said through the walkie-talkie. Even with the distortion, it was clear his words lacked Rory's southern boy casualness and that the voice was The Fallen One's self-important growl.

"They're headed for the gun. Switch targets, now," Teeks said, releasing the button on the side of the walkie and tapping Lumbra on the shoulder. "Bring up camera fourteen," he said to the man seated in front of the control panel, then depressed the button to talk to Rory again. "Take the south path and keep the cabins between you and the woods. They're running around the long way. And try to let the campers know where you're going to be. Over."

"Roger, Roger," Rory said, joy in his voice. For that moment he was just Rory, slipping out of character.

Onscreen, from the shadowed doorway of Deer Cabin, The Fallen One burst over the threshold, waving his hands over his head. He was yelling something to the campers, lost in the audio distortion caused by his flailing arms, but less than half of them turned to listen and even fewer followed him around the side of the cabin.

With his bulk, it was easy to think that Rory wouldn't be able to run, but he found the energy somewhere.

Daddy Teeks returned the radio back to the table, clipping it into its charging deck, and turned back to Kimberly. "You see?" he said. "All fixed."

"Not really. He's still there." She pointed to the main monitor. Ivan Butinelli was down on one knee now, but still the campers were keeping their distance. Four of their own were on the dirt now, at least one of them fully dead, possibly more, but it was hard to tell from this distance.

"Just because we can't hear Rory doesn't mean that they can't. He told them to follow him and they will. Either the fight will end or they'll get bored in a minute or two and move along."

"But not before he's dead and who knows how many of our *customers* with him. I can fix this," she said. "Let me go out there and talk to them."

"You see what I see, things are about to get much more dangerous out there. You can't control everything. Who knows? Maybe this is a blessing in disguise. Look at the campers and the way they're participating. Do they look like they're going to be asking for their money back?"

"No, but how many of them can we stand to go missing?"

This gave him pause.

Daddy Teeks wrinkled his nose at this and she could see him trying to think of a reply that made sense. Yes, at first they had only been selecting attendees who didn't have any families or strong community connections (at least from what they could tell online). But they'd vastly underestimated what the demand to attend Blood Camp Con would be among married men and twentysomethings who still lived at home.

Unlike their guests, who had all been selected through a much more rigorous screening process, a good percentage of campers were living much less invisible lives. Some of those men in white masks had people out in the real world who cared about them.

"Five minutes and I'll run back here," Kimberly said. "No one will follow me. I'm very fast."

Daddy Teeks rubbed his temples, watched on screen as Butinelli felled another camper, a girl this time. Who knew that a lifetime of fucking and stage fighting would translate to this kind of martial ability? Even though there had been no actual betting, she'd still gone out of her way to make odds for the "Who Will Survive and What Will Be Left of Them?" Poll. It was only for fun, but Kimberly had put Ivan Butinelli down at 4:1.

2:1 had probably been closer to the truth.

Keith Lumbra winced at another savage blow delivered with the stone. The improvised weapon was now so slick with blood that Butinelli was holding it in both hands to keep it from slipping away, like a bar of soap.

"Fine, go but do it quickly and be careful," Daddy Teeks finally said. "Send them all to the Head Counselor's Cabin if you can."

She already knew what she had to do. And she was already halfway out the door before he'd given her permission.

♦

Ivan saw the black t-shirts and white masks around him turning to react before he could make sense of the words.

It was a female voice, high and shrill, a girl's falsetto.

Oh baby, gonna make you scream.

"No," she yelled. "Stop it!"

Gonna make you cream. You'll like it. Oooo, yeah. That's good.

All of his fluids were pumping and the thing that most reminded him of was fucking.

He felt the drip of his own blood against his face like a strong sweat, but he did not feel the pain anymore. He was in the zone.

Ivan pushed the fat fuck's head into the ground with one hand and used the side of the rock to flatten his ear against his skull. He hit the tubby kid until blood welled up from his ear canal, the final toot becoming a little geyser.

After that, he decided to stop and move onto whoever else was thinking of coming within swinging distance.

"You're all on camera and we can see your numbers!" the girl yelled out, closer now. "Don't hurt him!"

For all the participants of the brawl, it was like she was speaking in code. But a moment after they had a chance to decipher the words, the shadows around him began to recede.

Ivan whirled and there was a girl there, pushing through the loosened circle. The crowd was already breaking up as campers turned tail to run from him.

Her?! She'd saved him. But wasn't she also in on it?

The blood that had leaked down and blinded his left eye had stopped stinging like salt water, but maybe that numbness was a bad thing because now he could only see out of the right.

You like it rough. Dirty girl. Mind if I choke you? Knock on your back door?

Ivan wondered how long he'd been packing the erection he felt rubbing up against his leg. He stood from his knees and felt it poking at him, the head rotating. Was the hard-on an automatic reaction to the exertion or had he actually been turned on by fighting for his life against a bunch of mallrats and cosplayers?

"Oh Jesus. Are you okay?" she said, giving him a once over. "Please, please, we have to get out of here," she said, beginning to sob before the second "please."

"You," Ivan heard himself saying. He raised his stone but realized halfway up he was too tired to wield it effectively, so he let his arm fall and the momentum spun him so he caught a glimpse of the orange sun before hitting the ground.

"I had nothing to do with this. I just want to go home," the girl, Kimberly, said. She started to cry as she kneeled down to cradle him.

Where had his rock gone? The fuzzy thought came and went as he realized he was safe. For the moment.

He let her help him up, his legs and arms somehow able to work even though his mind felt diffuse and sugary, like cotton candy pulled to its most fibrous and allowed to melt.

And as the two of them marched—not towards the road but deeper into the camp—he was almost sure that there was a crack in the air, like distant thunder. It was a clear afternoon.

Chapter Twenty

Back in the cabin, when nobody was looking, Gina had helped herself to the last of her vodka.

When she'd finished it, she wondered if it really had been a *secret* stash, because she'd thought she had brought enough for the weekend. But it was only Friday and already her second plastic flask was empty. The flasks were sold online and designed to help kids on spring break smuggle cheap booze onto cruises to avoid pay bars, but the containers were lighter than bottles and if you checked your bags on a flight then the TSA wouldn't bother them.

She would have shared, but there wasn't much left and she had needed the drink.

Now she was wishing she'd shared. Gina Bright had maybe overmedicated with vodka.

"It's so hot," she said between wheezes. She wasn't exactly trashed, that wasn't really a state she could enter anymore, and it had been years since she'd vomited from nausea brought on by drunkenness. When she was plastered she thought this resilience to getting sick was a good thing—that it meant she wasn't drinking as much as she used to— but when she sobered she realized that her supernatural tolerance just meant that her alcoholism was entering its final descent. The landing gear on Gina Bright's life was down and ready for tarmac.

Neither of her co-stars responded to what she said about the heat.

They were both too busy combing through the cabin. Clarissa Lee took the rifle down from over the fireplace and pulled back the lever to reveal an empty chamber.

"There," Clarissa said, indicating the desk wedged in one corner, "the drawer."

Gina lifted up the fabric of her shirt to fan the sweat from the small of her back.

Since Clarissa hadn't said which drawer to check, Marcus Lang started pulling open desk and nightstand drawers at random.

Gina tried to take in her surroundings as he did, but found it too dark in the room. She removed her sunglasses and found it easier to see where she was. Clarissa Lee's lodgings were much better than what Gina was sharing with the rest of the girls. Or. *Had* been sharing with the rest of the girls.

Your room doesn't matter now, some floaty, rational part of her brain started to remind herself, *now that they've started killing you all*. But the voice was quickly squelched as Gina's eyes focused on the easy chair, then the frilly duvet cover bunched at the end of the bed, and finally the stone fireplace.

Twenty years of losing work because the producers wanted a bigger star than Gina Bright, sometimes settling for Clarissa Lee, and this was where her life was going to come to a close: in a world where Clarissa Lee was still demonstrably a bigger draw. At least among the horror movie crowd.

A pocket of gas opened somewhere inside Gina and worked its way through chambers of her stomach and gut. Maybe she *was* drunk enough to puke.

"I'm just going to get some water from the bathroom," Gina said. She said it to no one, apparently, judging by their lack of reactions. They'd written her off. And they'd probably done it with good reason, as they must have known she'd been drinking. But that didn't stop her from resenting them.

She wiped a hand over her forehead and was surprised to find her bangs plastered there, sopping wet. That much salty wetness couldn't have been good for her dye job.

On uneasy feet, she navigated around Clarissa Lee's unmade bed and into the private cabin's small bathroom. *Oo la la. Her own bathroom.*

"Here, I got them!" Marcus yelled from behind her, the clatter of rifle shells in a cardboard box filling the room.

Gina Bright closed the bathroom door against their celebration.

The cool water from the tap helped focus her vision and calm her stomach. And so did the fact that although Clarissa Lee had been given a nicer cabin all to herself, her bathroom was still as cramped and unspectacular as the one Gina had been sharing with Margery and Tammy.

The washroom smelled like construction and there was dust from unfinished drywall ringing the sink fixtures. If this was what "recently refurbished" looked like, then she would have hated to see the old bathroom.

Gina bent, ran some more cool water over her hands, and circled a wet thumb around the faucet to clean away the dust.

There: that was better.

She looked up at the mirror just in time to watch her own reflection warble and then burst outwards.

Glass and two large, gloved hands shot out to meet her. The hands grabbed her sweat-slick hair in strong fingers and pulled her neck down to meet the teeth formed by the shattered mirror.

◆

Guns, like cars, were not something Clarissa Lee was able to see the appeal in.

She understood that there was a big market for these interests, for learning every piece of minutia one could about a favorite weapon or foreign automobile. But none of it interested her.

Even still, she knew where she'd recognized the gun from, now that she was cradling the weapon in her arms and pulling open the chamber.

This was a gun that had been a standard among hunters before she'd first met it, but was now famous in horror circles after she'd used it onscreen in the final act of *Death Birth* to send her own mutant child to oblivion, in the process opening a dimensional rift and ushering in hell on earth. No, that movie had not had an upbeat Hollywood ending, and that was why many fans liked it.

The rifle was a Winchester Model 70 with standard bolt action and added scope.

"Can I see it?" Marcus asked, his palms out to her.

It was a natural question. Over the last few hours, Marcus had confidently slipped into the role of leader for their little group. But that didn't mean that he was allowed to carry the gun, her gun. Especially after asking in such a half-hearted way, like it were only natural that she—the damsel—would hand it over.

"You can see with your eyes, not with your hands," Clarissa said, meaner than she wanted to, then added: "I know how to use it."

And she did. *Death Birth* had been Boyd Haight's first modestly budgeted picture and his last with Clarissa. Her ex-husband, perhaps already over the tipping point of self-indulgence that would lead to their divorce and the diminishing quality of his later studio films, had requested Clarissa go through two weeks of weapons training during pre-production. Her character was the wife of an avid hunter, thus needed to know how to handle the weapon. In the film, the subtext ended up being that: as macho as her husband was, he was still capable of being cuckolded by dark supernatural forces. It was a slight tweak on

Rosemary's Baby's marriage dynamics, but still more than a cheap rip-off.

Boyd had made the case that she should know how to handle a weapon. She hadn't paid much attention then, but it really was all muscle memory, once the Winchester was back in her hands.

"Cartridges," Clarissa said, holding her hand out.

She could tell that taking charge and refusing to give up the gun was doing something to Marcus, squashing a fledgling crush, perhaps? *That would be flattering*, she thought, giving Marcus a look and allowing it to be a little victory in the horror. *Not bad for an old lady.*

Whatever his hang-up was didn't matter. He gave her the box and she opened it, crossing the room to spread the bullets—ahem—the cartridges, out on the desk. There were five. Five rounds of Winchester .243 caliber ammunition, one round shy of the rifle's full capacity if you kept one chambered. At least she wouldn't have to worry about reloading.

It was amazing how the training she didn't think she'd been paying attention to came back to her, nearly thirty years after her shooting lessons. It was the only time she'd ever fired live ammunition, and she prayed that she wasn't loading in blanks right now. She wasn't *that* much of an expert that she could tell the difference between real bullets and fakes.

Before she began to guide the first round into the chamber, she looked up and checked out the window.

The action was interrupted by the sound of glass breaking in the bathroom. Gina Bright started to scream and was abruptly stopped.

"Hold on!" Marcus yelled, diving over the bed to the bathroom door and grabbing the knob.

"Don't," Clarissa screamed at him, meaning to say *"Don't open that fucking door yet, wait for me"* as she fumbled to get a second round in the gun.

But it was too late.

Chapter Twenty-One

In Rory's opinion, archery kills were completely underrated and underutilized.

True, there *were* slasher movies in which the killers used guns. Think of the shotgun blast to Tom Savini's head in *Maniac*. But those were few and far between, and when guns did get drawn by a slasher, it felt like cheating.

Bows and arrows didn't feel like cheating, at least not to Rory. He'd used bows to hunt, and the things were damn difficult to get a handle on. It took a combination of upper body strength, breathing, and steady hands to send an arrow where you wanted it, even if you were using an expensive, state-of-the-art compound bow.

Jason had hand-delivered an arrow once, but it was only in the remake that he ever shot a bow. As much shit as that movie got, that didn't mean an arrow still wasn't a cool way to get a kill.

And that went double if the bow was used to deliver a sudden, unexpected death with not even a musical cue to alert the audience of danger. No shrill piano jiggling, just a *thunk*.

There was something so surprising about a well-placed arrow.

He bet Marcus Lang would agree.

Lang opened the bathroom door and his eyes went wide at all the blood that must have been running down from the bottom of the mirror over both the sink and tile. Rory had dragged Gina Bright's neck down into the glass and sawed, stopping only when he'd hit bone. After that was done he'd let her fall away into the bathroom when he heard someone coming.

Marcus Lang looked up from the mess and through the window made by the broken mirror, straight into Rory's face.

Rory guessed it was dark enough in the hidden room that Mr. Lang couldn't really see him. The small room was completely black except for the red LED on the camcorder.

It would be best to put him down before Mr. Lang could see what Rory was preparing to do.

He loosed an arrow and it hit Marcus Lang at the base of the neck, to the left side, the shaft gliding neatly up to the fletching.

Rory had meant to put the arrow through his brainpan, but like he'd said: bows were tricky, even at close range.

Mr. Lang crashed against the half-open door, back and away.

Time to clean em up, Rory thought with grim satisfaction.

♦

Keith Lumbra was hurting.

He'd wanted to ask Teeks for another Advil, but that was before Kimberly had made a scene and left the safety of the control room to go unfuck the situation that had developed with the porn star.

Now may not be the best time to put in a special request. Teeks seemed preoccupied with worry…off his game.

"What is she doing?" Teeks asked, but the question must have been rhetorical because they could both plainly see what Kimberly was doing. She was helping Ivan Butinelli get to his feet after chasing off the majority of the campers.

"And what's going on—holy shit! Is that two kills?" Teeks was now watching the bottom row of monitors. "Tell me we have coverage,

Lumbra."

"I've been recording the cabin, main room and bathroom. And Rory's POV is still set to broadcast straight to the second tower even when it's off-screen. We'll certainly be able to cut something together," Lumbra said, feeling too much like a hero for someone who was bragging about getting comprehensive 'coverage' of two murders. As if it were his conscience's way of punishing him, his frontal lobe throbbed when he was through talking. His headache hadn't gotten any better once Kimberly left.

For the last few days, Keith had been trying to throw the pronoun 'we' into any statements that referenced the future. He was doing this to gauge Teeks' reaction. He needed to see whether the man intended there to *be* a future for Keith.

Unfortunately, so far he hadn't been able to tell anything. Teeks and Rory could have been planning to kill him as soon as filming was wrapped or they could intend to keep him around for the second annual Blood Camp Con.

"Actually. Lang's still moving," Teeks said, leaning in over the monitors for a closer look. Keith watched him without making it obvious he was looking directly at him.

They were coming to the end of the game much earlier than anticipated. Keith was less interested in what was going on with the camp and more with how he would go about executing the dire endgame decision he'd reached only seconds ago.

He'd never witnessed Michael Teeks this focused. Never this out of control. Add to that how occupied Rory was, not to mention far away from the control room...

And then thinking about how alone they now were, in here without Kimberly...

Teeks looked over at him. His boss had been saying something while Keith had been daydreaming.

Keith forced himself to focus on his lips.

"The campers, stupid," Teeks repeated. "They're migrating from Osprey to Lee's cabin and for some reason Kimberly's after them. Even though the fucking gun's about to go off." Teeks pointed down at the top row of the keyboard, to the row of numbers and cameras Lumbra needed to dial in. "Follow them, asshole!"

Keith got it together and held down the shift key and then 'one, four' to go to the establishing shot of the camp. Under his fingers, the keyboard felt more solid than it had in days. They'd locked him up and were making him work with antiquated equipment. But maybe that was for the best. One of those newer Bluetooth keyboards would have been too flimsy, insubstantial.

Before Keith could brace himself, Teeks used his hip to roll Keith's chair out from in front of the monitor. The keyboard clattered along with him, stuttering across the table under the pressure of Keith's fingers.

With the camera so far away, the subjects were small in the frame and Teeks leaned in, taking the mouse from Keith to work the zoom, rolling the trackball around with one finger to get close enough that the image was beginning to grow pixelated.

"Kimberly's talking to Butinelli but I can't tell what she's saying. She's gotta be playing the innocent. She's got to be telling him—"

Keith had reeled back with the keyboard and connected with Michael Teeks' jaw, keys out.

Teeks didn't look overwhelmingly hurt, simply surprised. The keyboard had been heavy, but not heavy enough. Or maybe it had only seemed heavy, weak as he was.

"Now?" he asked Keith. "You try this shit now?"

Oh God. What had he done?

♦

Clarissa bent near the bed.

The blood was dripping down Marcus Lang's chest, mixing with what was left of Margery Clampton on his shirt, but the blood didn't gush.

Not gushing was a good sign, right?

"Jesus," Marcus said, holding the wound with two fingers, arrow still in place. "Do I pull it out or leave it in?"

Clarissa was resting a hand on his shoulder. The contact was partly intimate, partly utilitarian: she'd just finished dragging him out from behind the bathroom door, throwing it shut so no more arrows could be sent into the room.

"Leave it in, for now," she said.

Her other arm was filled with the gun, fully loaded now, the stock rested against her knee.

She alternated looking at his wound and out the front windows. From crouched down low like this, using the bed as cover, she would only be able to see anyone approaching the cabin if they were tall and stood inches away from the glass.

The sounds of activity, footsteps and a door slamming, filled the small cabin and they weren't coming from either of the doors they could see. There was the crunch of gravel close to the cabin, but the sound dampened as their stalker transitioned to grass and then stopped completely.

The Fallen One had left the building, through whatever secret means he'd used to get in. But his retreat may have only been momentary.

"There's a room in there, behind the mirror," Marcus said, now that it seemed okay to talk. He looked down to try to see how bad he was hurt. He probably didn't get to see much. All he managed to do was bump the tail of the arrow with his chin, sending a hot wave of pain through his nerves.

"Can you stand?" she asked, removing her hand from his shoulder to pull the bed sheet out from under the heavy comforter. She wrapped the fabric around her arm so she could stay low, reeling the sheet in like a fishing line. This lady did not mess around. She looked worried, panicked even, but she wasn't giving up and there was something else in her voice and manner: exhaustion?

Marcus took the ball of off-white linens she was offering and pressed it down, hard around the end of the arrow.

"Yeah," he said, but he had his doubts. He also worried that when trying to walk he was going to trail some of the sheet like a cape and end up tripping, but he wasn't about to ask Clarissa to go into the bathroom to find a towel. "But," he said, thinking, "you need to pull it the rest of the way through for me."

She nodded at this, and the fact that she needed absolutely no convincing made Marcus feel a flicker of concern for her mental health. This could be what a nervous breakdown looked like, or, since she was so ready for action—and it pained him to think this—she could have been in on the entire act. Consider her cushy private lodgings, the fact that she hadn't traveled in with them.

He shook the thought away. That was paranoia and sudden blood loss talking.

"Sit up," she said, waving him up from where he was leaning against the bed frame. He couldn't see what she did but he certainly felt it. The fletching almost tickled as it pulled through, a downy feather to the damaged ligature of the base of his neck and a weight lifted off of his collarbone.

There was no spurt of blood once the arrow was pulled through, so that seemed like a positive.

"He's out there," she said in a whisper, peeking over the bed. It was unclear to Marcus whether she could actually see The Fallen One, or if this was just a working hypothesis. "So, what we're going to do, is slam the bathroom door like we're barricading ourselves in here, but what we're really going to do is run out the front door, then to the woods like you wanted to. Originally."

Marcus nodded to show he understood, but nodding with a dime-sized hole drilled into your neck was a bad idea.

"We stand, I'll slam, and then we run. Okay?" she asked, repeating the plan while speaking slower. He hoped she just thought he was stupid, not that she thought he was dying of blood loss.

"Yes," Marcus said, using his words this time. The sheet was beginning to feel wet under his fingers. He applied more pressure, clamping down to try and cover both the entry and exit wound in his fist.

She brought her gun up and counted down with three fingers. He couldn't remember having ever seen her in any movie where she played a cop, but it'd be a shame if she never got to explore the role. She'd clearly be good at it.

Marcus stood and experienced a moment of weak knees, like both of his legs had fallen asleep, but quickly recovered.

Clarissa didn't slow down to wait for him. She slammed the bathroom door and took long strides to the exit, keeping her eyes on the window that overlooked the rest of camp.

Feeling the strength come back into his legs with each step, either adrenaline or the numbness of death, Marcus limped after her.

She looked to him, her eyebrows cinched up in a question: *are you ready?* She had the gun braced against her hip as she reached for the knob.

"I'm right behind you. Go," he said, more as an exercise in feeling like he had any influence over the situation, because it was clear that she was proceeding with or without him.

Clarissa Lee stood against the wall, swung the door open and into the room, then turned to face out the doorway.

She fired the rifle immediately.

◆

Keith Lumbra's vision was fading, his lungs paradoxically feeling like they were too full of air instead of straining for it, which they certainly were.

What was he leaving behind? Would dying here, like this, ensure his legacy as an underground artist, a gore-hound provocateur? Would his films receive a surge of popularity? High profile re-issues that came with documentaries explaining the strange real-life crime he'd been tangled up in before his death? Or would he leave behind nothing but a few bad movies on sloppily authored DVD-Rs, movies that would die along with the format?

Teeks had two hands around Keith's neck, successfully choking the life out of him.

Then the sound of the gunshot made Teeks' grip relax enough so Keith could catch a quick breath. It was a soft pop by the time it made it across campus and through the walls of the control room, but it was unmistakably a firearm.

Roaring his frustration, Teeks swung his arms and sent Keith— and his rolling office chair—careening into the edge of the mixing table.

The monitors and hard drives wobbled against the impact, but no equipment fell over.

"She's shooting," Teeks said, nearly screaming at Keith with frustration. Teeks searched the secondary monitors for a clear shot that would let him see what was going on. He picked up the keyboard from where it had landed after Keith had smacked him with it and cursed down at the numbers. It looked like a few of the keys had popped out when Keith had used it as a weapon.

Instead of offering to help, Keith used the arms of the roll chair to lift his ass from the seat and throw his weight onto the table, aiming for the hard drives.

"No!" Teeks said somewhere behind him, but Keith was already balling up AC cords and Ethernet cables in his hands, plucking out what he could with his minimal leverage.

Teeks tried kicking the chair out from under him to get him onto the ground, but Keith had too good a grip on the end of the table, had his fingers locked in place. All the kick ended up doing was tugging the bike chain taught around his ankle as the chair flipped off its wheels and clattered to the floor.

Once all the hard drives were disconnected, the disks hopefully suffering gigs of data loss or at the very least some file corruption, Keith swiveled onto his belly. He was weak from the beatings and subsequent infections, but glad for the weight he'd lost during his time with Rory as his personal chef. Keith Goldman hadn't been this skinny since grade school.

Keith slapped the walkie-talkie and its charging dock and watched the radio collide with the wall.

There was another gunshot outside and Teeks couldn't help himself from turning to the monitors to see what was happening, even as Keith was pulling out component and s-video connectors, the table finally giving out under him.

As he fell, Keith made sure to pull the televisions down onto both of them.

Through some miracle, none of the glass of the screens had broken. The room was coated in a green static glow, the light of the cathode ray tubes from the older monitors reflected off the walls and ceiling.

If there were any more gunshots. Keith couldn't hear them. He was too busy caving Michael Teeks' nose into his skull with a trackball mouse.

Chapter Twenty-Two

Nate had read a lot of essays, a lot of "think pieces," about fandom. Many of those authors had viewed fandom as a series of compulsive acts. Some of the newer theories claimed that being a fan of something wasn't about *the thing* itself, at all, but was instead about filling a hole in the fan. The way a stamp collector cares very little about the image on the stamp, merely that they own the stamp.

But that was all bullshit.

Nate's fandom wasn't about compulsions.

It was about sacrifice.

Those sacrifices may have *fed* his compulsions, but it was the sacrifices that had molded his life into its current, depressing, shape.

Take for example his brief marriage and endless divorce: it was his wife or his hobby. Supporting both would have been financially untenable, and it was beginning to get to the point where there would be no more hiding the expenses or his collection.

So, he'd made a sacrifice: he chose his hobby over his wife.

And the compulsions were there, for sure, but he'd never been able to make the leap from torturing animals purchased from the "Small Friends" section of Petco (hamsters, mice, etc.) to bigger game like dogs or cats. And never people. Oh, he'd thought about it plenty, but he'd never done it.

The people with him at this camp seemed to all share a fandom, but theirs was different. They seemed to enjoy the fake stuff, the slasher movies and heavy metal music.

Nate was a little more of a square than that. Even after his divorce, when he could have dressed however he wanted, his closets were still stocked with polo shirts and button downs. He kept a tidy push-broom mustache and wore bifocals that made him look a little bit like the BTK killer. And the resemblance was not accidental.

No, the express fandom this new convention was supporting may not have been *his* bag, but as an admirer of Dahmer, Gacy, et al. he could enjoy the acts he was witnessing.

It didn't matter how you dressed it up: murder was murder, and Nate had now witnessed a couple of murders in the flesh. For years there was never a way to tell if the videos he was finding online were actual snuff or just special effects, but there was no faking what was going on at the camp.

Yup, that was Nate: square and old school.

He'd heard of the deep web, but hadn't the guts or occasion to try logging in himself. Until someone in one of his chat rooms had explained what the con was going to be, then told him that "going dark" was the only way to buy tickets for the event.

And now he was here. First in line to watch the finale, actually, ready to see an aging movie star was eviscerated in front of his eyes.

Nate had sacrificed a lot to be here, but as the day was nearing its end he felt refreshed. He felt that when the weekend was over, he'd enter the world reinvigorated.

Maybe on the drive home, he'd pay his ex-wife a visit.

All Clarissa Lee had to do was open that door.

♦

It wasn't a mistake, shooting the camper dead after she yanked open the door, but it hadn't been Clarissa Lee's best case scenario.

She worked the bolt and watched the gold glimmer of the spent cartridge fly out the side of the rifle.

At least the gun worked and the bullets were real.

There was no movie magic to shooting a human being in real life. Clarissa had hit the guy center-mass, close to his heart. The blood didn't show up well on his black t-shirt, but the camper twitched with the impact of the shot and then fell flat on his face.

"Back up! Get away!" Clarissa yelled to the rest of them, waving the barrel in small, controlled circles. The shot was still ringing in her ears, so she screamed the words and tasted blood from the exertion.

There were maybe seven or eight campers. It looked like they'd been fanned out in front of her cabin, expecting to creep up to the windows for a show, though they hadn't yet worked up the nerve.

They all listened, backing up and raising their hands.

One of them broke the golden rule and addressed her: "Don't shoot!" He didn't do anything as cinematically bombastic as piss himself, but he sounded like he was close.

"Marcus, are you good?" She yelled without turning around. She was not taking her eyes off the campers. Some of them were muddy, their pale forearms mottled with blood from where they'd been fighting with Ivan Butinelli.

"Yup." He sounded weak. That or she couldn't hear as well as she could a minute ago.

She caught the movement as three of the masks turned like satellite dishes. They were turning to watch the side of the cabin. They were seeing something approach that she couldn't hear through her tinnitus.

She turned on her heels. Sneakers had been a good choice of footwear. They afforded her maximum mobility.

The Fallen One was keeping low to the ground, his stride

elongated enough that he looked like he was doing a series of lunges, working out. The big man was carrying a fireman's axe, his elbows up in front of him, readying himself to swing or chop wood. Where was he getting all of these different weapons? She tried to imagine all of the horrible things hidden in the camp and surrounding woods that they hadn't seen yet.

The Fallen One made the mistake of going for Marcus first instead of her, which presented Clarissa with a straight shot once he changed his mind.

Hubris? An underestimating of a woman? Or just a horror fan's inborn respect for the conventions of the slasher film? *Leave the final girl for last...*

She fired, the bullet connecting with The Fallen One's shoulder and knocking him back but not down.

He was six feet from her now and still coming. She estimated he was about one second from being able to reach her with the axe.

Ideally, she would be able to work the bolt in less than a second.

She fired a second time, catching him low in the chest. Right in the solar plexus chakra. You learned these things, living in L.A.

Inside the open square of his mask, his mouth moved. She couldn't hear him gasp, she was fully deaf now from the three gunshots.

The Fallen One lost his forward momentum until he stopped completely. The head of the axe pulled him down to earth. His grip only loosened on the handle once he'd hit the ground, sprawled on his back and still.

◆

It was so much worse than Rory'd anticipated.

And to think, he'd wanted to practice *this*.

Teeks had claimed that they didn't want to ruin the costume, but maybe he'd just been looking out for Rory's well-being. Teeks was smart like that.

Getting shot was no game, even with a couple of feet of Kevlar stitched into your jacket.

Rory's ribs felt like they'd been shattered by the second shot. As much as he wanted to, he tried not to breathe. He kept his mouth slightly open, like he was dead and his face had frozen that way, with his lips parted.

Gasping for air through his mouth would give him away.

We want to give the impression of the supernatural, Teeks' words came back to him.

Again: Teeks was smart.

Every part of The Fallen One's costume had been bullet proofed. So even though giving the guests live ammunition *seemed* like a risk, it wasn't much of one for Rory.

Yes, all he had to do now was lay still and wait for Clarissa Lee and Marcus Lang to leave so he could sit up, resurrected, a couple of bullets pancaked to his chest, and then pursue.

Yup. Just lay and rest.

The air seemed to clear of the post-gunshot quiet and Rory could hear the crush of dead grass under feet.

Any minute now he could take a big gasp of fresh air. He just had to keep holding his breath. It would taste so good. Maybe if he chanced a small sip in through his nose…

"You never walk away from these fucks without being sure," Clarissa said to someone, standing over Rory now.

Wait. Standing over?

There was a third gunshot, this bullet tearing through Rory's open mouth at such an angle that it chipped three of his teeth as it scrambled his brain inside of The Fallen One's bullet-resistant mask.

◆

Kimberly the P.A. appeared across the clearing, surrounded by a group of campers who had backed off when they saw the gun.

She had one of Ivan Butinelli's thickset arms slung across her shoulders and was crying and screaming hysterically.

"It was supposed to be a game! Like paintball he'd said!" she screamed, then she seemed to spot Clarissa for the first time. The girl put a hand up. "Don't sh-sh-shoot!" Kimberly stuttered and bent low in order to make herself a smaller target.

Without Kimberly's support, Butinelli slumped to the lawn and groaned.

It seemed to Clarissa that the girl had enough of show business. That was probably a record for how quickly she'd seen someone disillusioned.

"I know, I know," Clarissa said, trying and failing to make her voice sound soothing. "Now, how do we get out of here?"

Epilogue

Kimberly knew Daddy Teeks was dead the second she saw Lumbra running towards them.

He didn't even have to say anything, the gauze on his face was soaked through with too much blood. Blood that was too fresh to have been his own.

He didn't have to, but he did say something,:

"He's dead! Fucking dead and you're next bitch!"

Ms. Lee used her fifth and final bullet to shoot Keith Lumbra before Kimberly could even scream for her to do it.

The heartache of knowing her lover was dead made it even easier to pretend to be shocked and saddened with how Blood Camp Con had turned out. No, acting the part wasn't much of a stretch at all.

Lumbra's quick execution was a silver-lining on an otherwise dark cloud. If he said *anything* more incriminating, he could have spoiled everything for Kimberly.

"Rory—the big guy—he's the one who drove the bus in," she'd told them once she calmed herself enough and she was sure they trusted her.

By the time they'd backtracked to the body (Kimberly had to be *sure* he was dead, too), she was sufficiently composed enough to volunteer to dig through Rory's pockets looking for the key.

It was good to have a break from carrying Mr. Butinelli. Both he and Mr. Lang required assistance. Kimberly would be amazed if they were both able to make it to the nearest hospital alive.

On their way back to where Rory had stashed the bus, Ms. Lee waved the gun at any campers they encountered. She was acting like she still had bullets and they believed her: after all, she was a professional actress. Yesterday, Kimberly didn't think she could have been any more in awe of this woman, this star, but she'd been wrong.

They were able to board the bus with no issue, aside from a few campers who wanted a ride. They somehow were convinced that this was *still* a planned part of the weekend and couldn't see why a ride back to the airport was an imposition.

There were no safety belts in the reclaimed school bus, but Clarissa and Kimberly did their best to brace the two injured men against each other in their seats so they didn't roll off onto the floor.

Kimberly said she'd watch them if Clarissa felt up to driving.

As they drove by the sign that assured them that Camp Rockwogh would see them next summer, Kimberly Yost tried to think what her next move would be.

Two options presented themselves:

In one she stuck to her story of claiming ignorance as to the true nature of the Con.

In that future, Michael Teeks and Rory... Rory... whatever his last name had been... they would become household names, and, if anything, she would become just as recognizable as the fourth survivor of the Convention Massacre.

It was highly unlikely that she would be linked to any of the crimes as an accessory. Her and Daddy Teeks had done their due diligence well in advance. In this future, Kimberly would be the Squeaky Fromme of modern fandom.

After the initial media coverage died down she could write a tell-all book. She could even do signings at horror conventions, depending on how tasteless her and her representation wanted to go, playing off the deaths of so many.

That first choice provided a bright future, but it somehow felt like a betrayal of Daddy Teeks and the legacy they'd been trying to build with the con.

The second option was to scour the internet to find like-minded help building the Second Annual Blood Camp Con. You heard it time and again from organizers, but: the first years of these kinds of events were always filled with growing pains. If anything theirs had been a moderate success.

Kimberly would be able to perfect the formula on the second attempt, she was sure of it. Money wouldn't be an issue, since she knew she was provided for. Daddy Teeks had showed her how to access his funds, in case of emergencies.

It would be easy.

Now that she looked over at them, she could see that Misters Lang and Butinelli were losing consciousness fast. All she would need to do would be to come up behind Clarissa Lee and slit her throat.

She'd secreted away Rory's pocket knife when she'd bent to search his pants and jacket for the bus key.

It was a harder decision than she thought it would be. Door number one or door number two? Instant fame or honest work? A slasher movie with a soft, PG-13 ending where far too many of the characters lived? Or an appropriately downbeat one?

Both options were so enticing.

She would have to make her decision soon, before anyone realized their cell phone was out of range of the jammer.

She was such a fan of Clarissa Lee. But, then again, she did want to leave her mark on the genre…

What to choose?

Acknowledgements

This book, for better or worse, would not exist if it weren't for a complicated web of support (both direct and indirect) from a litany of friends, mentors, and collaborators. There are probably too many people I owe big-time for me to list them all, but the major-est of major players are: John Skipp, J. David Osborne, Tod Clark, Jeff Strand, Shane McKenzie, Paul Goblirsch, Stephen Graham Jones, Scott Cole, Cameron Pierce, Matt Serafini, Gabino Iglesias, Adam Howe, Bracken MacLeod, Armand Rosamila and Blu Gilliand. Big thanks to George Cotronis for his beautiful cover (http://www.cotronis.com/). Love to the lovely Jen, for not kicking me out.

And final thanks to you, dear reader, for making it this far through the book. If you liked *The Con Season* and wanted to leave a quick review, I'd be even further in your debt.

Want More Cesare? Read on to get your fix:

Download a FREE exclusive ebook
by visiting www.adamcesare.com

The Blackest Eyes is a mini collection of two short stories. This ebook is free for everyone who signs up for *Adam Cesare's Mailing List of Terror*.

What are you Waiting for? Go to AdamCesare.com and sign up today!

ADAM CESARE

VIDEO NIGHT

BE KIND REWIND

SAMHAIN

Also Available:

Video Night

"If you put together the gore, action, monsters, and sense of excitement that made '80s horror movies so great, you'll only have about half of what makes *Video Night a must-read tome for horror fans.*" –**Horrortalk**

"The momentum keeps building. The stakes keep escalating. The monsters just keep getting worse and worse, the catastrophic mayhem more juicy and hopeless. Best of all, the writing moves like a greased torpedo, compulsively readable as it rockets through your brain [...] Adam Cesare's gonna be a Fango superstar." – *Fangoria*

"Video Night is a sharp, smart, energetic novel which pays tribute to all the brilliantly gross horror comedies of the VHS era, even as it carves out its own corners of shock literature." -*Daily Grindhouse*

THE ITALIAN CANNIBAL HORROR CLASSIC!

WARNING! BANNED IN 28 COUNTRIES

ADAM CESARE'S

TRIBESMEN

Also Available:

Tribesmen

"Sick and sardonic and just plain brilliant." **- Duane Swierczynski, author of *Fun & Games* and *Canary***

"The best new writer I've read in years. Wonderfully lean prose and edge-of-your-seat thrills. Drop everything else and start reading *Tribesmen*." **- Nate Kenyon, author of *Day One* and *Sparrow Rock***

"A cunning, cinematic redmeat feast for weird film lovers and horror freaks, Adam Cesare's *Tribesmen* is a first-rate literary midnight movie, and a blistering debut. BRING YOUR FRIENDS!" **- John Skipp**

"*Tribesmen* is a gory and clever homage to those Italian cannibal flicks that we all love so dearly, but without the real-life animal cruelty! Highly recommended." **- Jeff Strand, author of *Pressure* and *Wolf Hunt***

"Sometimes everything goes wrong, in the best possible way. Think *Snuff* and *Cannibal Holocaust* meeting at a midnight movie. And then give one of them a camera, the other a knife." **- Stephen Graham Jones, author of *It Came from Del Rio*, *The Gospel of Z* and *Demon Theory***

This novella is available in ebook, audiobook, and paperback.

ADAM CESARE

THE SUMMER JOB

SAMHAIN

Also Available:

The Summer Job

"The prologue of *The Summer Job* is one the best and scariest openings to a horror novel I've ever read. [...] The rest of the novel is equally great. It's a little like Jack Ketchum's *Offseason*, if you replace the cannibalistic savages with a satanic cult, but I feel so strongly about *The Summer Job* that I'll go out on a limb and say that I believe it's better than *Offseason*. I really do." **—LitReactor**

"The textbook definition of a nail-biter. *The Summer Job* is a kissing cousin to inbred classics from masters like Ketchum and Kilborn. Cesare's best novel yet" **—Bloody Disgusting**

"Cesare's latest is a knockout...There's a potent retro vibe running through Cesare's work, in general—he's the closest thing literary horror has to its own Jim Mickle or Ti West." **—Complex**

Check out this novel in ebook and paperback.

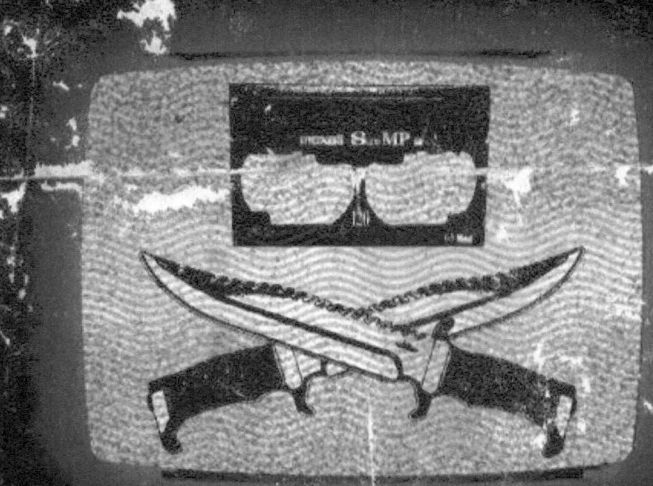

Also Available:

The First One You Expect

"The First One You Expect is a fast, sexy, fun, dangerous read, and enough of a taste to make me hope Cesare ventures into crime fiction regularly." **-Spinetingler Magazine**

"An engaging, contemporary thriller with a cutting-edge narrative, and characters so real they could live next door." **-Rio Youers, author of** *Westlake Soul* **and** *Point Hollow*

"[A] hugely entertaining parable of the be-careful-what-you-wish-for kind." **-Crime Fiction Lover on their "Top 5 Books of 2014" list**

This novel is available in ebook and paperback.

MERCY
HOUSE

ADAM CESARE

Also Available:

Mercy House

"Adam Cesare's *Mercy House* is a rowdy, gory, blood-soaked horror tale guaranteed to keep you up at night. And if that was all it was, I'd have been a happy reader. But Cesare has a maturity far and away beyond his years. His characters are treated with a surprising capacity for understanding and empathy, giving them an unexpected depth rarely seen among the nightmare crowd. *Mercy House* is the kind of novel you sprint through, eating up the pages as fast as you can turn them, and yet it lingers in the mind like a haunting memory, or the ghost of a smell. Cesare is poised to take the reins of the new generation. Looking for the new face of horror? This is it right here."—**Joe McKinney, Bram Stoker Award–winning author of *The Dead Won't Die* and *Dead City***

"*Mercy House* is 100% distilled nightmare juice. Adam Cesare notches up the horror to nigh-unbearable levels. Even my skin was screaming by the end of this book."—**Nick Cutter, author of *The Troop***

"Adam Cesare makes his presence felt with *Mercy House*. A no-holds-barred combo of survival horror and the occult."—**Laird Barron, author of *The Beautiful Thing That Awaits Us All***

"This is extreme horror at its best, so don't step into this book with an uneasy stomach. You must wait sixty minutes after eating before opening up *Mercy House*."—***LitReactor***

**This novel is available as an ebook
from Random House Hydra.**

Also Available:

Exponential

"*Exponential* is fast-paced fun, a rollicking monster movie in 200 quick-moving pages.»
-Ain'tItCool

"*Exponential* is an excellent novel, one of the best creature features I've read in years, and will very likely appear on my Top 10 Horror Reads of 2014..."
-Horror After Dark

"...Adam Cesare's mix of grim violence and old school horror movie references make for a great read."
-Rue Morgue (#152) on *Exponential*

Pick up this novel in ebook, audiobook or paperback.

THE ARCADE SCENE
ISN'T DEAD...IT'S ALIVE!
ZERO
LIVES REMAINING
ADAM CESARE

Also Available:

Zero Lives Remaining

"The victims in *Zero Lives Remaining* are different--far from being the typical lost, wide-eyed fodder, these outcasts and obsessives quickly catch on to the truth of their awful situation and come to battle armed in their own strange ways...enough to leave every joystick of the arcade drenched in blood." **–RUE MORGUE**

"While *Video Night* is an exceptional novel,the wistfulness in Cesare's latest, *Zero Lives Remaining*, is twice as thick, the monsters a tad more gooey and intelligent, and the pacing even more insane. The result is a narrative that oozes a bizarre kind of melancholy while celebrating the classic video games and music of a different era while crushing bodies with more speed, creativity, and ease than most current best-selling horror authors put together." **–HORRORTALK**

"Cesare is on the top of his game and delivers possibly hisbest story yet by unleashing a fountain of energy to keep you turning pages and enough horror to make you think twice about touching another arcade game." **–SPLATTERPUNK MAGAZINE**

"I've yet to read an Adam Cesare novel that didn't A) immediately reach up from the page, grab me by the Dennis Rodman lapels, and pull me facefirst into the story, or B) get me to fall head over heels for this world before I'm even a quarter of the way through the book." **–STEPHEN GRAHAM JONES,** *Mongrels* **and** *The Last Final Girl*

This novella is available in ebook, paperback, and audiobook.

♦

For more titles and news about upcoming work be sure to visit AdamCesare.com to sign up for the mailing list or find Adam on Amazon

About the Author

Adam Cesare is a New Yorker who lives in Philadelphia.

His work has been featured in numerous magazines and anthologies.
His nonfiction has appeared in *Paracinema*, *The LA Review of Books* and
other venues. He also writes a monthly column about the intersection
of horror fiction and film for *Cemetery Dance Online*.

His novels and novellas are available in ebook and paperback from
Amazon, Barnes & Noble, and all other fine retailers.

Please visit his website adamcesare.com to learn more. Author photo by
John Urbancik.

www.ingramcontent.com/pod-product-compliance
Lightning Source LLC
Chambersburg PA
CBHW020633250626
47154CB00008B/2651